JOHN E. TYO

6

JACK'S
BACK

outskirts
press

About the Author

John E. Tyo is an avid reader and loves to write stories for people of all ages. A retired English professor, he has published in many genres but prefers writing adolescent and young adult novels which deal with positive themes and life lessons. John has been involved in sports all his life. He enjoys playing basketball, handball, touch football, swimming, surfing, and golf. He was born, raised, and lives in Southern California.

Plot

The background of this story is about Jack, a fifteen year old boy who feels isolated and alone. He uses sports to help him feel relevant in his high school which in his eyes consist of the "in group"the popular kids versus the kids like Jack who are not. He feels second best at home surpassed by an older brother who bullies Jack to get his way. Jack's hard working mother, Sally Marston, is bullied at work as well. Jack encourages Sally to stand up to her tormentor but he realizes he needs to follow his own advice. The story is complicated by the fact that Jack is actually being accepted and cared about by one of the more popular girls at school, a cheerleader named Annie. As life becomes more complex and Jack receives more acceptance because of his athletic ability, he is faced with a challenge that might allow him a permanent ticket into the "in group"and Annie. This decision is going to affect many and Jack must decide who he really is and what really matters to him in life.

Characters

Jack

The title character is fifteen year old Jack. He perceives himself as an outsider. He feels like he is always observing people but never part of the group. He sees himself as second best at school, sports, and home. He desperately wants to change this situation but doesn't know how. He sees a glimmer of hope to belong at school but can he do it?

Grant

Grant is Jack's older brother and the opposite of Jack. Grant has confidence in abundance and enjoys exerting power wherever he goes. He is used to being a bully who gets his way and chooses to put himself first in most situations.

Sally Marston

Sally is Jack and Grant's hard working single mother. She is unhappy in her job and her home life. She is very lonely and tends to allow herself to be bullied at work because she is the sole support of her family. She wants to stand up for herself but doesn't have the courage to do so.

Annie

Annie is a cheerleader and sees Jack in a different light than Jack sees himself. Jack can't imagine that a super popular girl like Annie is interested in him but there is a strong attraction between them that can't be denied. Jack's lack of confidence and fortitude might spell disaster for their relationship. Jack must understand who he is and what he needs to do to prove it.

Jared

Jared is an extreme competitor of Jack's. Jared, a popular, aggressive person, is street smart, and believes bullying and manipulation are the ways to achieve his goals. Jared devises a plot to get rid of Jack and also a nemesis that he blames for his suspension. Will Jack become his puppet to stay in the popular group and hope to retain his relationship with Annie?

Coach Sijohn

The high school basketball coach helps define what it means to play as a team. He knows unselfish teamwork will win games. He recognizes Jack has what it takes to be a top player if Jack can step out of his own shadow and take chances on the basketball court and in life.

Mrs. Bramhaus *alias* Broomhead

Mrs. Bramhaus has the fierce eyes of a raptor, someone who lives off of weaker animals. Sally Marston's boss takes pleasure in keeping people in their place... especially the people that work under her at the hospital.

CHAPTER 1

"LEAVE ME ALONE,"JACK said from under a blanket. "I'm not getting up until you get out of here."

"You'll get up now."Ms. Marston's eyes flashed at her son's covered head. Curtains were swept back from the window. Jack struggled to one elbow. White light invaded eyes still glued shut.

"That's more like it. What's the matter with you today?"

"Nothing,"said Jack. Then, to see how much she knew, "Just something at school..."

"At school? You're not in any trouble?"

"I can handle it, Mom. I'm a big boy."At least soccer news hadn't trickled down into his home yet.

"I know you are,"his mother said. Jack didn't believe her, but she went on anyway. "Sometimes family can help..."

"Yeah, you can help. Get out of here so I can put some clothes on,"he said in a kidding voice. On the way to the door she said, "Without me, you'd sleep twenty four hours a day."

"Fat chance,"Jack mumbled, blinking at the light flooding through the window. Jack sat up, stretched, and sighed. Had the loss of the soccer game just been yesterday? Was it all a bad dream? Jack felt he had let the entire team down... especially himself. The fact that he was unable to block that last play was so hard to bear. If the first string goalie hadn't been injured Jack would never had blown that last block. If only his team-mates knew how hard he had tried.. if only the school knew how badly he had wanted to be the hero of the last game of the season. If only... if only just doesn't count.

On the bright side, he reminded himself, the sea-son's over. No more practices and no more games. He kicked the door shut.

The only thing left for soccer players was the team party at Annie's house. She was a cheerleader. Jack thought about her for a minute, then crawled back into bed. The last play kept running through his mind like a movie reel stuck on a continuous loop. His mother's voice jerked him back to reality.

"Jack, will you get out here? Your breakfast is get-ting cold."

He automatically slid out of bed and into jeans. His mother had disappeared by the time he reached the kitchen, but breakfast was on the table. She swept back into the room when he was on his second scoop of oatmeal.

"You're making me late for work."

"I need my sleep,"Jack answered sharply.

"So do I. But there's other things in life... like making a living... and going to school."She made them sound like equally despicable things you had to do.

Jack moaned like he was sick. "Isn't there a flu virus going around?"

His mother slapped a hand on his forehead- a shade too hard for Jack. "You're not warm."She squinted at him suspiciously. "What is the matter with you?"

"Nothing, I guess."

"Then get going. No use both of us being late."His mother reluctantly hooked her purse off the chair. She wanted to go to work about as much as Jack wanted to go to school. The necessity of it put her back in a bad temper. "Don't bother thanking me for breakfast."

Jack didn't bother. The room was suddenly tranquil. He always knew when his mother was home by the amount of words in the air. He teased her about the noise, but missed it, too.

She was right about one thing: he'd be late if he didn't hurry. Soon his bike was cruising down the farm path to school. Not many took this trail, especially so early in the morning. He dodged pools of irrigation water bordering the beaten-down road. Halfway there he saw "Bottoms Up."

That's what the kids called it. A gorge was deep-cut into the soft ground. Its ledge curved around in the shape of a beer bottle. The bottom was deep enough to scare you, but it was only wide on the south end. With enough red-hot speed, the narrow end could be jumped by a biker taking off from a ramp. That is, if anyone was crazy enough not to be spooked by the canyon looming beneath. Everyone called it Bottoms Up for obvious reasons. The farmer, not fond of law suits, periodically ripped down the jerry-built ramps the boys built for motorcycle jumps.

Mark Lowe tried to jump the ditch on his bike last spring. He came up a little short and catapulted into the ravine. Mark had not really died, but his bike did. He ended up in the hospital; the bike lay inert at the bottom of the abyss. The caliper brakes poked up like antlers of a forgotten hunting trophy.

Jack edged carefully around the brink. There was not much room on the sides of the trail. The path widened after the ditch into an easy corridor bordered by eucalyptus trees. Lettuce was growing in the fields this time of year. Bent backs wavered in the distance over helmets of green.The gray block of Kennedy appeared from around the trees, a yellow light glowing from a window. It was still too soon for other students to be there yet. Jack had a "zero"period language class. It was not required, and only offered forty minutes before the actual school day started. He climbed up the steps to reach the plateau of buildings. The school was asleep. Automatic street lamps still gleamed in the new morning light. The custodian had not even raised the flag yet. Jack stopped when he reached the classroom with the glowing yellow window. A bespectacled man answered the knock on the back door. The room had the chalky smell of school about it, unmistakable as medicine in a doctor's office.

"Buenos dias,"the man said. "Glad you could make

it."The voice was thin and reedy like Mr. Martinez himself and teeth showed when he smiled. Jack grinned sheepishly and merged into his desk with the rest of the students. No detention would follow. Teachers of zero period used sarcasm, not detention, as weapon of choice. Too much hassle and students drop. Time was soon lost in a confusion of Spanish verbs.

Jack lingered after class when the bell rang. There were still a few minutes to socialize before period one. Mr. Martinez taught English, too, and always had papers to grade. Jack was treated as a trusted affiliate, often helping with pages from his own class. This time he set to work transferring marks into a grade book.

He didn't mind--they usually talked as they worked. Besides, it was cool outside and there were plenty of people who saw the last soccer game. It was quite a bit warmer inside. After awhile, Mr. Martinez looked up from an essay.

"You were mentioned in The Outlook today."

Jack blocked his face with the grade book. The school paper would make him the goat of the soccer season. Now everyone who wasn't at the game would know. Excess copies sometimes were dropped off at his Mom's hospital. His brother Grant, an alumnus, even had a copy sent to him at the college.

"We got second place again, huh?"

Jack emitted a plain "uh huh"from the papers shoved in front of his face. His voice sounded strained. Mr. Martinez got the message and changed sports.

"You know basketball starts soon."Another gap came for Jack to respond. This time he didn't grunt.

Undaunted, the teacher tried again.

"Didn't you win the intramural free throw contest last year?"

"Yeah... but I didn't make the team."

"You've grown,"Mr. Martinez said, encouraged by finally making the conversation two-way. After another lapsed moment, the teacher said, "You're closer to the basket now."

Jack coughed, then mumbled, "Made a mess of the last game in soccer. Doubt if they want me to go out."

"I don't understand."Mr. Martinez blinked from behind his glasses. "Who are they?"

Jack shook his head. The teacher was analyzing his words as if they were written on an essay.

"The coaches?"

Jack didn't answer.

"The players?"Mr. Martinez blinked at him.

Jack still didn't answer. The teacher blinked at him again.

"The spectators?"The wire frame glasses slipped down his nose. The eyes stopped blinking. "Who are you afraid of?" Martinez peered curiously over the clear lenses.

Jack pushed the grade book back. There was no easy answer. The bell rang and saved him from the silence. Five minutes to get to class. His locker was across from the PE building, all the way on the other side of campus.

"See you tomorrow,"Jack said. Then in deadpan teasing, "I'll be late again."

"You better not be," the teacher said with false threat.

When bells rang at Kennedy everybody moved--mostly into one another. Waves of students surged inside the school buildings. Jack saw Jared in the swarms heading for first period. He was laughing; the smile faded when he saw Jack.

The flurry of humanity diminished at the PE building. That was one advantage to having a locker so far away. The disadvantage was sometimes being late to Chambers' math class. The bell rang just before Jack slipped into the back row.

Miss Chambers usually took a while to get her act together in first period. While the class waited, Jack noticed Annie and Tara buzzing near the front of the room. Being cheerleaders, they had both been at the last game.

Annie's long hair was variegated shades of light and dark brown, most of it mixed to the same dark honey color of her eyes. She turned around suddenly and stared at Jack. Although she turned back just as quickly. Jack was grateful when Miss Chambers finally called the class to order.

CHAPTER 2

THE NEXT DAY wasn't much different from the day before. With soccer over the school days blended into successions of bells ringing students from period to period. The weekend came closer, though, and Grant was due home Sunday.

His older brother was quite a contrast to Jack. A bit of Grant's legend was still enshrined on a wall in Kennedy's gym: wrestling champion for two years running. Jack wished a bit of the magic had rubbed off.

The last time home he had hitched a ride on the back of Grant's motorcycle. They had whipped through farm trails with Jack hanging on for dear life, a plume of dust spewing behind like rocket exhaust.

Unfortunately, the most permanent thing that rubbed off that day was dirt. Grant pranced back to college; Jack was bestowed the laundry as a smelly souvenir. To quote his mother, "Life isn't fair." But it was predictable, anyway--it always began with the same shrillness.

"Jack--get up! Time to go to work."Then less loud, in a grudging voice: "I'm not your alarm clock."

But she was, unfortunately. The charge of his mother's voice caffeinated his nerves. His toes twitched to life. Warm feet contacted cold floor. Without actually deciding to do it, he stepped into the dreariness of a new day.

The adrenalizing effect of his mother had worn off by zero period. He could relax at school, taking refuge in daydreams. Martinez caught him in the middle of one; the teacher honed in on vacant eyes. The day-dreamer was hit with a wake-up call-- a question he had barely heard.

Jack couldn't find a Spanish phrase to soothe the teacher's temper. This time--favorite or not--he didn't have a choice about staying after class. Fortunately, the guise of strictness on Martinez's face went out the door with the other students. When he saw the old friendliness return, Jack went on the offense.

"School's boring,"Jack told him. "Study the book or study the notes, then take a test on it. I forget it the next day."

"Sorry if we don't entertain you,"the teacher said, blinking up a storm as usual. "You've got us mixed up with the internet."

Sometimes Martinez sounded too much like a parent. But the day was different in Miss Chambers' class. She'd be the last person Jack expected to do anything new.

First the class was divided into six groups. Jack heard himself called after Matthew Chen. Then, a chunk of a math problem was assigned to each section. Each small group would huddle to figure out their piece of the puzzle. The total solution required all answers to fit back together. Miss Chambers called it "jigsawing."

The straight rows dissolved into small wheels of students. Matt scanned the problem, but most just talked. Jack was sketching on some paper when Matt came up with the answer.

"Time's up!"Miss Chambers called. "Remember, every group must have an answer, not just your own. Get busy and share some of that knowledge."

Matt split them up to interview the other clusters. Jack approached a wedge of people in the corner. Annie was sitting on top of her desk instead of in it. She spoke before he could open his mouth.

"Sorry,"she whispered. "We're still working. Do you have your answer already?"

"We have Matt." That was explanation enough. He was the smartest in the room, Miss Chambers included. Jack also sat on top of a desk as he tackled Annie's problem.

For once, the clang of the bell startled him. They still hadn't found the answer. Jack was trying to help, but only Annie seemed interested.

"We'll continue tomorrow,"Miss Chambers announced. Bodies were already streaming out the door. "Class dismissed,"she called at their backs.

Jack had to admit he liked studying that way. At least you met new people. For a change, he even looked forward to math. Unfortunately, he was just a little late the next day. He silently slipped into his desk, hoping not to be seen.

Then it happened again. Annie and Tara stopped talking to watch him sit down. The rest of the class continued to chatter. Jack was mystified--nobody else noticed him. If they had, it might have attracted Miss Chambers' attention.

The rest of the period was one long standardized test. The jigsaw method was mothballed--like most good ideas at school. The test demanded concentration, and again he wasn't ready for the chime of the bell. Sighing at an unfinished problem, Jack bent down to scoop an extra pencil off the rug. Pointed, short, suede boots turned their points toward him.

He waited, but the shoes didn't move. He had a hunch who they belonged to but his eyes had nowhere to go but up.

Ankles...

Calves...

Knees...

He got to the thighs with what was left of an innocent face. When he confirmed it was Annie, and the fact that she was standing still looking back at him, a line of blush rose from his neck like a rising water mark until his scalp tingle. He wished he wouldn't do that.

Jack could see Tara hanging back a bit, but the rest of the class was gone. He did a pretty good intimidation of one of Mr. Martinez's blinking attacks. This wasn't jigsawing: Jack had nothing to talk about. Dropping his eyes, he saw an envelope dangle under a polished fingernail. Finally Tara blurted from behind:

"Oh geez, give it to him! We're going to be late."

Annie coughed a laugh and slid the envelope into Jack's hand.

CHAPTER 3

THE SOCCER FAILURE burned into Jack's mental retina like a nightmare--which was just what he was having on Saturday morning. Even in dreams, the last soccer game ended the same. If only he had been quicker to block the kick that won the game. If only his opponent had not been so fast. If only the moon was made of cheese. Saturday morning reality was a relief after Friday night dreams.

A slamming door told him his mother had left for work. It was another not-so-subtle reminder to get moving. She couldn't stand for him to sleep, even on Saturday. Jack stumbled into the bathroom, and on the way out spied a note taped to the dresser. It was in his mother's sparse printing.

Jack,

Since this is your day off, here's a list of things to do. Remember, your brother will be home tomorrow. I want everything done. First of all, the laundry... and you could help your brother by doing the yard...

Jack stopped reading. Some day off. He crumpled the paper in his fist, then spread-eagled back across the bed. After a while, he roused himself enough to toss it at the wastebasket, but it curled off the edge. When he went to rebound it in, he noticed the basket had been emptied.

Suddenly awake, Jack jumped into his pants and went outside. The big trash barrel was outside for collection, brimming with garbage. Annie's letter was on the top, floating in a sea of potato skins. On the way back to the bedroom Jack blew on it, as if that would cleanse it from impurity. So much for hiding it in a place nobody would look. Sally Marston was nothing if not conscientious about trash day.

In contrast to his mother's stern hand, the envelope was addressed in fluid strokes produced by the broad tip of a calligraphic pen. There certainly was no mistake: his name stood out in flamboyant relief, the letters tipped by broad curlicues and flourishes.

JACK MARSTON

He had never liked his name before, but now it didn't look half bad. His eyes jumped around suspiciously on the way back to his room, as if he had counterfeit currency instead of a perfumed letter.

He unfolded himself back on the bed and tapped the envelope against his finger. A card fell out and winged open on Jack's shirt. He flipped it up and glanced down the front of it. Cherubs danced about, zinging heart-tipped arrows at each other. Cupid's victims were zonked into delirium over their wounds.

Jack wished he felt as good. The inside of the card

invited him to a party-- the team party for soccer. It was at Annie's house next Saturday. R.S.V.P. requested.

The back of the card was dominated by two words. The first word said "LOVE" on the top and the second word "ANNIE" on the bottom. The invitations had been printed on some computer program that made it have even more elaborate script than on the envelope. By comparison, the second word was understated in regular blue ink. A postscript said simply, "I hope you can come." Jack was picturing that possibility when a banging on the front door brought him back to the present.

He thought about not answering but quickly stuffed the card back in the envelope. He glimpsed at the waste can, decided against it, and slid the invitation between the mattress and the box spring. The banger was getting impatient. When the door was finally opened, his brother brushed by.

"Forgot my key,"Grant said.

He stumbled in dragging a large sack and a backpack. Although older than Jack, he was four inches shorter. Grant made up for that discrepancy, however, by outweighing his little brother by a bulky thirty five pounds. There was no doubt who the wrestler in the family was.

"Don't just stand there,"Grant commanded. "How about a little help?"Jack wrapped the laundry bag around his elbow, frowning at its weight--it would take more than one load.

"How long you here for?"Jack asked.

"Long enough to get that done."

"Good,"Jack said, "and you can do the yard."Grant didn't seem to hear.

The door swung back open, blown by a gust of wind. Jack dropped the bag and went back to shut it. A gleaming motorcycle leaned to one side of the driveway. It was a dual purpose 250cc Enduro with knobby tires and an electric blue tank. Street-legal, yes, but made to have fun in the dirt. It was a powerful off-road bike, but still light enough for jumps. He didn't hear Grant come up behind him.

"It is nice, isn't it,"his brother said.

Jack agreed. Grant stood for a moment longer in admiration, then strode out the door waving his keys. Jack was about to turn around when his brother called to him.

"Wanna go for a ride?"

It didn't take Jack long to decide. He straddled the cushion and positioned his feet on the pegs. The bike came alive. Grant twisted the throttle; Jack seized his brother's waist to keep from sliding off the back. The acceleration could bounce heart against spine.

Jack felt the wind blow-dry his face; then a blast of air made it hard to breathe. In a few minutes, the glide of pavement bumpety-bumped into potholes. The familiar farm trail blurred beneath the big tires. Jack leaned forward and screamed:

"This is private property."

Grant turned his head sideways and grunted.

He gave the handle an extra twist and his passenger lurched into the backrest. The front wheels sailed into a wheelie and they gaped at the sky. When the front tire struck earth again, Jack was aware of bicycles ahead. Some boys were practicing jumps over small wooden ramps they had built. The bikers rolled back at the roar of the 250.

Bottoms Up loomed ahead, with poor Mark Lowe's bike glistening up from the underside. Ramps were at both ends, but the boys huddled at the narrow side. The ramp at the wide end was an exercise in fantasy-- no one would make it unless they were born with wings.

Especially not loaded with two people. It was too much weight to risk over a bike eating hole. Just ask Mark Lowe. Just ask Jack.

Grant didn't ask.

Instead he twisted his right hand again. The full throttle snapped heads back. Jack hunkered down in his seat, squeezing his brother's ribs. He could have broken Grant's ribs he squeezed so hard. Then all either could see was sky. The big cycle, up on it's back wheel, shot for the wide end of the gulch.

"He's going for it,"a boy on a bike said. The others pedaled ahead, competing for a closer view. Grant turned his head sideways again.

"Hang on!"he shrieked.

The bumpety-bump of the tires ceased as the motorcycle hit the ramp. Jack felt his stomach tighten, then the lift of flight, but this time he shut his eyes to the sky.

CHAPTER 4

ENGINE TORQUE WHIRLED the back tire in a hopeless airborne search for something to grab. The brothers appeared in a dust cloud, poised over the abyss like an indecisive storm. The audience of bicyclists pedaled forward, straining to see through obscured air. The drive wheel slammed down first, just on the edge of doom.

The tip of the ledge disintegrated; so did Jack's stomach. The knobby tread of the dirt bike threshed the soil away like a revolving claw. Then Jack felt traction bite into the cliff wall. The cycle shuddered sideways--a hesitation only the riders felt--then revved them up and over onto flat earth.

When the front wheel knocked down, a cascade of whistles burst from the caucus of bikes. Jack opened his eyes and mouth in wonder and thanksgiving. Some dust spewed in and he coughed it out. His brother's hand left the throttle to wave at the crowd.

They executed another wheelie in front of the boys

on the way home. Grant waved again like a rock star saying goodbye. His little brother basked in reflected glory as they rode into the sunset. Jack liked the spotlight. It was secondhand glory, but glory nonetheless.

The adventure came to an end when they reached home. Grant disappeared into the heat of the bathroom. Jack was left with a sack of smelly body wear. His heart was still running fast like a revving motorcycle. His brother came out to toss his cycling clothes on the rug. They made their own dust cloud.

Jack's jeans were the same shade of brown. He stripped and added them to the pile. Business as usual in the Marston house. Jack was just about dressed and ready to go to the laundromat when Grant's cell phone rang. Jack grabbed the vibrating cell.

"Hello is this Grant?"a voice asked, melodious as a purr from a cat. Before Jack could answer, Grant snatched the phone.

"Get lost,"he said to his brother.

Jack did, without comeback. How could he complain after that cycle flight?

Grant's lips were still glued to the phone when Jack returned with the laundry an hour later. Now his brother was purring like the girl, albeit in deeper voice.

Jack dragged in the clean clothes and started jamming them in drawers. The feline purr quit in the other room. The bedroom door kicked open.

"Just give me mine,"Grant said, not looking at his brother. "I have a date."His nose went into his backpack. "Hey, do me a favor..."

Jack didn't answer; Grant didn't notice.

"Tell mom I had to go. I've got a test at school." Already he was toting the backpack toward the door.

"What about the yard?"Jack called after him. "That's your problem."Grant went out the door as if he didn't hear.

The 250 rumbled and Jack was alone again. After a moment, Annie's invitation was pried out from under the mattress. He propped it on a bookshelf overlooking the bed. The fancy printed letters looked down on him like a promise he couldn't keep.

Sally Marston was dragging when she arrived home from the hospital that night. The starch of daybreak had disappeared--her body now shrunk into an old lady's crouch. Her tired face showed exhaustion and her blue scrubs were wrinkled from too many hours immersed in other people's problems.

He told her about Grant.

She seemed to disintegrate at the kitchen table. She neither checked to see the chores were done nor talked as she placed the fast foot stacks on the counter.

"I don't understand. Didn't he leave a message?"

"I told you, Mom. He just stayed a few minutes."

"Tell me again. It's not like your brother."

Jack told her again and Sally's eyes filled with tears. She poured a glass of wine and looked dully at the liquid. "This has been a really hard day and I was hoping to see Grant to brighten my evening."

"Hey, what about me?"Jack questioned.

"Of course, you too, honey." Sally responded, "But Mrs. Brumhaus was so mean today and I try so hard."

Jack said roughly, "Tell her to get off her high horse..."

"I can't do that."

"You'd tell me, and not quietly."His mother's voice, when she really used it, was louder than anyone he'd ever heard.

"She's my boss. You're my son."His mother was suddenly defensive. "Look, everybody in the world suffers. I hate my job, but I do it."

She tipped back to take a drink from the glass. When her face came down, the chin was out, defiant. Her mouth was sad.

"I finished my work and I left."

"What about Brumhaus's work?"

No answer on that. His mother poured out a second drink. He caught her eyes beneath the stem of the glass. Sadness seemed to have won over defiance. Jack made a try at comfort:

"This isn't the only hospital in town."

"I'm used to Memorial."She pushed the drink back and whispered, "If old Brumhaus would disappear..."

"That's not going to happen,"Jack said.

He could meet his mother's reality head-on. In this sense, they were good for each other. They were a family, just the two of them. Of course he didn't have to confront Brumhaus. It was easier to give advice than to take it.

"I'm sorry Mom,"Jack said sympathetically.

"Me too,"Sally sighed.

Sally Marston glared. She placed her wine glass loudly on the table. But then, from rock-bottom rancor, her demeanor blossomed into a condescending smile.

"You're so young, honey,"she said.

He hated it when she talked like he was five years old.

"You are only fifteen,"she said. "What could have happened at your age?"

A certain soccer game flashed through Jack's mind. He remembered the chill when the final gun sounded; the silence of starters marching by him as if he didn't exist.

His mother laughed softly, as if reading his mind. "You worry about soccer games... and parties."

"What party?"he said instantly. A rosy pink began to burn, like a wick burning down to dynamite. When his head was entirely red, he accused her with explosive power:

"Have you been in my room?"

"The invitation..."His mother smiled like the cat that ate the canary. "It was printed so pretty. So fancy..."

"It was my business."

"And my job's your business?"She beamed that infuriating smile again. "Jack, you threw it away. It was too pretty to throw away."

Jack scowled into his empty plate. "I wasn't throwing it away."

"I see. It was just resting there in the trash."She waited for Jack to explain, but he didn't. Then she said, "Are you going?"

Jack wouldn't look at her.

"It's R.S.V.P.,"his mother said finally. "That means you've got to let her know."

That information brought her son's head around.

"In person,"Sally Marston said. "That's the polite thing to do."

CHAPTER 5

BOTTOMS UP DIDN'T seem as lethal on Monday morning. Jack walked his bike carefully around the pit. He kicked the platform that had launched the 250, as if to pinch himself about a dream.

The boys had been busy, evidently inspired by Grant's flight. Another small ramp had been constructed on the neck of the gorge. Even that slender stretch seemed beyond the jumping range of a bicycle. No doubt about it: even the narrows looked too far to fly over on Monday morning.

Ms. Chambers wasn't about to give Jack any angel wings: he was late again. Nothing new about that. Nor any surprise when Annie turned her head and smiled. The glance was stolen and furtive, and not only because of Ms. Chambers.

It was like he had a relationship with Annie now. He didn't know how that happened, how he deserved it. Math class stretched out ahead like the Sahara. No conversation of any kind allowed. Only teacher-talk, which didn't exactly qualify as equal human inter-change. Lines of equations wavered on the board until Jack's eyes went completely inward.

He thought of sports, this time basketball instead of soccer. Today was the first day of practice. It made the day different. He had decided the dead time that followed the end of the fall season was boring. His quick feet made him better at basketball anyway.

Jack imagined himself on the court. He could almost hear the swish of the net as he launched one from the top of the key. The referee shot his hand up: "Foul called..."Then the zebra flipped his wrist down: "Basket counts..."

The score was tied and no one could stop him. He heard the crowd chant his name from the sidelines.

Mars-ton

Mars-ton

Mars-ton

Then he was all alone for the fans to see, isolated for a freethrow. One second to go and the game on the line. He could almost feel the sweat drip from his face as the crowd hushed. Jack knew he could sink it--Automatic City. He dribbled once, then bent at the waist. The ball straightened in a frozen rope, rammed the heel of the rim, and shot down the net.

An opponent threw a basketball pass full-court as the buzzer expired. Jack felt himself rise on the shoulders of his teammates. The mania of the crowd broke off into a pattern. It was his name being chanted again from the sidelines.

"Mr. Marston."

Strange, Jack thought.

"Mr. Marston."

Why was there a "Mister"in front of it?

"Mr. Marston."

Miss Chambers voice yanked Jack from the shoulders of his teammates. She continued impatiently: "Please go to the board!"It was not a question; perhaps it had been the first time she said it. Jack unstuck his knees from the bottom of the desk.

Students murmured as they saw his reluctance. The mob is always pleased at the sight of blood.

"Put up the last equation,"the voice ordered.

The teacher knew he didn't know it.

The class knew he didn't know it.

Annie knew he didn't know it.

Jack went to the board, anyway. He picked up the chalk, glanced at Chambers, and waited for his ruin. Frost from the teacher's icy squint was almost tangible, like smoke over dry ice. Jack found a crack in the parquet floor that needed inspection.

"You won't find the answer there,"Ms. Chambers said.

Jack didn't look up.

"Don't you think it's time to join us and pay attention?"

"Yes, Ma'am."

"Sit down,"she huffed.

Jack shuffled back with his eyeballs still stuck on the floor. The faces in the room radiated delight: an oasis had been found in the Sahara. Giggles and smirks washed the room clean of seriousness. It was easier to concentrate on Jack than math.

Were Annie's brown eyes sympathetic? Jack saw her looking at him without seeming to look at all. Finally she turned around, too. It was forever before bells rang the end of first period; the day dragged on but finally it was time for basketball practice and he was suited and ready to run and jump.

Several players had already started a warm-up game. Jared, Dereck and Moe teamed against Eric, Ryan and Jamal in a half-court contest. It was a mismatch: Jamal was short and a freshman to boot. Long, rangy Dereck was the dominant force. It wasn't worth watching. Jack shot at the other end with the rest of the squad.

Soon Mr. Sijohn, dressed in a three-piece suit, strode through the boys. Except for blue running shoes, he looked ready for a business meeting. Erratic streaks jagged his crewcut like somebody'd gone crazy with a can of gray spray paint. He was shorter after school without the glossy, dress boots he wore to class.

Regardless of height, his erect posture reflected pride. The high bones of his Native American face prop his checks out like poles in a tent. He was a handsome man even when his jowls puffed around the whistle in in his teeth.

Phreet!

At once the balls were rolled to the manager, Dan

McGee. The freckled-faced boy sucked them into a bag not unlike Jack's laundry satchel. The team circled the coach at midcourt. He seemed to number their faces before speaking.

"There isn't much time between soccer and basketball," he said. You soccer players must adjust to a different sport. Quickness is more important than straight-ahead power." He numbered their faces again. "Our first game is in less than two weeks."

When he finished talking, the boys were divided into two squads. Jack as he expected, was with the poorer players. The shape of the ball had changed from black and white to brown leather; the hierarchy of the team, however, was set in stone. The best athletes in soccer would be the best athletes in basketball. It stood to reason. Jack would back up Jared again.

Jared stood out because of his size: weight not height. Although a couple inches shorter than Jack, he more than made up for it in width. His girth alone took up room under the basket, and he wasn't shy about using his strength. His sharp elbows could rearrange opponents like electric cattle prods.

Jared's trademark razor blade...Jack assumed it was dull..dangled from his neck on a glinting gold chain. The bulk of the body and flash of the blade lent Jared an unmistakable presence...identifiable from the farthest seat in the peanut gallery.

Jack soon found out he didn't have to sit during practice. The second squad was small but fast. Jack's name was yelled first when it was formed. The back-ups were even called "Marston's team."

Not that they came close to winning the daily scrimmages. But it did make Jack feel good, especially when they pushed the first stringers to the limit. More than once Mr. Sijohn called "Nice work, Jack." Sometimes he even barked it when someone else made a bucket. It was meant as praise for the second team, but the misdirection made Jack wince.

The week floated by in harmony. His communication with his mother was confused by the overtime she spent covering for Broomhead. His communication with Annie was limited by late arrivals and quick getaways. The party was a week from Saturday and he had yet to R.S.V.P.

At practices, Jack's name became synonymous with the enemy. The starters dreaded tribute to "Marston's team." Usually, a pungent proclamation about defense followed a plaudit to Jack: a compliment was perverted into a jab at the string. As a result, he was targeted for double-teaming defense. Whenever Jack slipped from Jared, Ryan slid over to help out.

As the season opener drew close, practices became longer. Jared emerged as the leader of the first string. No surprise....he was leader of the soccer team too. Not the best player...that was Dereck...just the leader. Soon the coach was calling for "Jared's team" to go up against "Jack's team."

The tussle between the two squads was fierce, if not always equitable. Dan McGee kept a running tab of the score from a table at midcourt. On Thursday, Jack's team edged ahead, which burned Sijohn's face. Jared and Ryan bore down, forcing the ball to Dereck because of the big man's height advantage.

"Don't depend on that in a game,"the coach warned. Dereck might be short compared to the other center." He summoned the the starters by blasting twice on the whistle.

"The key is team work,"he said to the five kneeling before him. "Everyone's a threat to score. That way nobody can gang up on one player. If they double-team, there's a man open. It's as simples as that. Give your team-mates the ball and they'll do the same for you."

"Someone's open,"Mr. Sijohn hollered as soon as play resumed. "Hit the open man, Jack."

Unfortunately, the seam in the defense vanished as quickly as it materialized. The coach clapped when Jack's man swiped the pass. Jared's eyes glimmered like stony black marbles, bouncing in self-congratulation between Jack and the coach. Sijohn gazed in approval when the team broke for the showers chanting:

"Teamwork..."

"Teamwork..."

"Teamwork..."

Then Jared the leader took charge of his flock.

"Who we gonna beat," he shouted.

The sheep roared back, "Oxnard!"

"Beat who?"Jared bellowed.

"Oxnard!"

"Who?"

"Oxnard!"

The cheering pulsated like the thump of a vibrating drum until the showers swallowed up the beat. Jack was still saying it to himself as he rode home that night.

CHAPTER 6

"WHAT DO YOU think of this?" Mrs. Marston asked. She slapped down a paper on the the kitchen table. Jack recognized the hospital letterhead, then the general idea that it was advertising a job. Her ambition caught him by surprise.

"Head Nurse? You wanna be Head Nurse?"

"Head Floor Nurse,"his mother corrected.

"What about old Broomhead?"

"She'd have a fit. I'd be her equal." A bloom of enjoyment blossomed in the lines leading to her mouth. "And on a different floor."

"Go for it !"

Jack flipped the paper back at her. His mother glowed at the prospect, the bloom flowering under tan makeup.

"No way,"she said. "I'd rather be a soldier than a general." She squeezed his shoulder. "I've got enough troops to worry about here."

She was flippant, but fringes of truth stuck to her words like decayed honey. She must have sensed it for the subject changed.

"Heard from your brother?"

Jack shook his head. It was her favorite question, and he was tired of it. No mileage in that line of conversation.

"What about the R.S.V.P.? Have you let the little girl know yet?"

"She's not a little girl." Jack cringed after he said it. Now his mother knew she was bugging him.

"What's her name?"

When no answer came, she dropped into a quasi-trance, like a psychic pulling a voice from the other side. Her stone faced son twitched in his seat. After an insufferable minute...insufferable for Jack, his mother was having a great time...she snapped out of the trance.

"Annie!"

She announced it mystically, as if divined from a crystal ball instead of an invitation. Her eyes danced at his. Jack tried not to smile. He left the table without a word.

Jack and Jamal meant at school the next day.They had become fast friends because of basketball. They thought they had arrived early for practice but realized Annie, Grace and Tara were there already practicing their cheers and cranking their arms in a dance routine. The first stringers warm up game had not even started yet.

Two men short, Dereck invited Jack and Jamal to

play. Both boys were surprised at the invitation and eagerly accepted the challenge. Nothing like a game to loosen the joints. All the warm-up in the world didn't approximate a man guarding you with something on the line. Moe and Jared finally strolled out from the lockers, too late for this game. They lounged on the bench to lace their shoes.

Jack faked Dereck off his feet, then snuck an arm under for a bank swish. The big center said "nice shot"under his breath and patted Jack's rump. Jared snapped his neck up with the riff of the net. Moe left the bench to shoot at the other end. Jared seemed to have a hard time stringing his shoes.

Jack took a pass from Ryan, faked Dereck back with a drive, then buried a jump shot from the base line. The net's sweet sound made Jared miss an eyelet. Jack repeated the same move with the same results.

From then on, Jared's eyes never left Jack. Head up, the first stringer poked his laces like a blind man. At this rate, he'd practice in socks.

Jamal was playing over his head, or rather under everyone else's. His game was more subterranean than alpine. He zipped through bigger boys like a blur. Eric finally switched to him. The starting guard was just as fast and aggressive.

He rejected Jamal's jump shot but fouled him, ramming his understudy to the floor. Jamal jumped up right in Eric's face. Eric pushed Jamal away. Tensions were high. Jack quickly stepped in. He knew Jamal would loose because of Eric's size and girth. Jack broke in shouting . His words were strong and clear.

"We are a team. Get your acts together. We want no trouble."

The boys eyed each other but tempers seemed to be soothed for the time being. The ball was in motion again. Competition was strong. The point of an elbow... Jack didn't know whose...speared him in the gap between the ribs. Play didn't stop, but Jack sure did. He doubled over with immediate sickness.

The game went on. A reaching hand flicked the ball into the hoop. Jack tried to jog back but stumbled like a drunk with dry heaves. Jamal delayed his dribble out high.

Be tough, Jack thought. Don't let it show...

His stomach wanted to come out his mouth. He gagged it back down, just barely. Sijohn stopped bellowing at the troops and squeezed his eyes into slits. His cheeks swelled around the whistle. Everything stopped.

Jack finally doubled over, straining to drag air through a pinched windpipe. It got easier, slowly. Oxygen dribbled in to replenish empty lungs. Nausea remained behind like a bad belly ache, but he was going to live.

"You guys stink,"the coach said. Nothing about the elbow. When play resumed, the two stacks of cards on Dan McGee's table lost their equality. The second stringers weren't close by the end of the practice. No one mentioned the cheap shot on the way to the lockers.

Athletes were tough...you were supposed to shake it off. Don't even rub. Then the other guy knows he hurt you. But then there is another unwritten rule:

Get back.

Get even.

Hurt him like he hurt you.

Maybe not today, but sometime. That is, if you wanted to compete...

Jack didn't know who his attacker was. Perhaps it was an accident. Lots of bodies under the basket. It was a teammate, after all, not an enemy. At last the ache in his gut disappeared.

His ears were wet from the shower when he and Jamal left the gym, first stringers not far behind. Laughter pulsed around them at some private joke. Jack's name was mentioned but when he turned the laughing stopped. The starters draped themselves over a picnic table outside the gym door. A gaggle of cheerleaders popped out of the girl's gym and trickled towards the boys. Jack had the feeling the timing was not accidental, on either side.

Jamal tugged on his arm. When they deployed forward, Jack noticed a girl detach from her clique. It was little Tara waving like submerged bait in a gentle current. The small guard bit the hook and was reeled away but he didn't let go of his friend's arm.

Jack found himself dragged to the table with his buddy who didn't want to talk..not to Jack, anyway. Jamal was using him for a six foot security blanket in case his conversation with Tara fizzled. Jack gaped around aimlessly. Jared was nearby talking to Grace, the Homecoming Queen during soccer season.

Jack turned to Jamal, who was soaring proudly

over Tara. Jamal had found someone shorter than he was. Then over both their heads...which wasn't hard to do...he fastened onto familiar eyes from Chambers' class. The eyes were dark, honey brown: they didn't turn away.

"Hello, Jack,"Annie said.

The melody of her voice was different than math class, less matter of fact. He nodded at her but couldn't think of anything to say. She whispered:

"I haven't heard from you..."

CHAPTER 7

JACK TRIED TO talk but his mouth just opened and hung there. Voices hung around them as couples stepped off together into the twilight. Annie's voice hushed, as if trying to create a conspiracy between them.

"I mean... about the party. It's Saturday night..."

Jack looked away for the first time, hesitating. "I'm not going," he said quickly, way too quickly. The speed of his words sounded like a brushoff. The sentence paralyzed Annie for an instant. She seemed to procrastinate full comprehension, dark honey-brown eyes asking why.

Before he could say, Jamal yanked on the security blanket. Having said goodbye to Tara, Jamal started to pull his friend through the yard again.

Jack didn't fight it. He turned to the gate to see Annie still frozen in the same spot. It looked like everyone else had gone home; then Jack saw a golden glint sparkle on the beach behind her. Jared had been watching them.

Needless to say, the next Saturday night was dismal. Jack kept telling himself not to think about the soccer party, but somehow television didn't quite cut it. Finally, he went into the kitchen where his mother seemed to have caught the same sickness. She said it into a coffee cup:

"Grant hasn't been home for a month. "Jack smirked, "His laundry has."

She considered that, not knowing if he was serious or playing with her. She finally said, "I could use some help, you know," she sighed. "You and me both. Grant hasn't done the lawn since..." Jack stalled not knowing how far back to go. His mother finished for him.

"Since Daddy left?"

His father's name wasn't mentioned in casual conversation...only in shadow, sadness and gloom. Jack tried to slip the deadbolt back into an invisible barrier.

"That's history, Mom."

"I don't need you to tell me that."All she needed was a truism from a second son. His father's ghost scraped sores that hadn't had time to heal -- that might never heal.

"I was going to say... "

"That people leave? I know that a little better than you."

She wandered through the clouds off her coffee cup for a time, then said, "They get tired of you... or there's somewhere else they have to go."

Jack scooted around to sit next to her. "I'm not leaving."

He put his arm around her protectively.

"Yes, you will."Her eyes glossed. "When the time comes, you'll go too."

"No, I won't."

"You'll discover college... or girls."

She burlesqued a wink. "The girls come first."

He thought of Annie and the soccer party. He could be there right now -- the guy who lost the season for them. He shook his head no. "You're sweet."Vibrato trembled into her voice. "But your father left one day. You will too."

"It's not the same thing."

"I know. You're my son not my husband. But it's the same..."

A surge of masculine guilt weld up inside, and interior flush he could not control. She went on like he wasn't there.

"People leave. Your father did it. Now Grant..."Her lip shivered. "They don't even say goodbye. "

"This doesn't go anywhere, mom."She was talking to herself now. His response just punctuated stops and starts.

"That's how it began with daddy. First, he stayed out all night then it lasted week at a time. Finally, he never came back. "

"Stop it, Mom"

"You know the hard thing?"The monologue dropped her eyes into guarded passages of the heart.

"I kept expecting him to walk in the door. Just like nothing happened. He'd ask, what's for dinner? And sit down at the kitchen table."

She picked up the coffee mug, then released it with a clack into the saucer.

"But he never came,"she said. "He just stopped coming back. I would've taken him back, you know. He was all we had. But he vanished from the face of the earth... Like he never existed. All we have left is his name."

Her eyes slid back onto Jack. "You were just a little boy."

"Not so little."He twisted his neck to say words that would sting

"Mom, even I knew dad drank."

"I did too, Jack. I still do."She warned him with a tremor, as if this was a family secret even family didn't discuss. Jack forged on anyway.

"It's different. He used to hide a bottle in the hamper."Mrs. Marston murmured, "My son the laundry man. "

She could explain what happened fine. A stranger would think she accepted desertion, dealt with it even. But the hurt was way too deep. A well of fear drained into the hole his father left, keeping it fresh and unforgiven. His mother said:

"You were so young then, Honey."

"I'm almost 16 now,"Jack sputtered.

They started the retreat from the danger zone. This was as close to truth as they got -- just dancing on the edge of it. Talk about the problem, complain about it, feel sorry for yourself but don't try to fix it. Stay stuck like a scratched record that only repeats.

His mother felt helpless, doomed to rerun the past over and over again in all relationships. She had the loudest voice Jack had ever heard. But she was too sad to speak for herself, even to Broomhead. She released him from the embrace and said:

"You haven't felt the bite of living yet."The familiar summation told Jack it was time to move away, time to tread safer ground that wouldn't divide and swallow them up. No one was allowed to close too long, not even him.

They had a truce the rest of the weekend: Jack didn't mention his father and his mother didn't mention Grant or Annie. Somethings were best left inside. Words cleansed and healed, but words ripped off protective scabs.

Jack was on time to zero period on Monday morning, to Mr. Martinez' delight. The teacher marked the occasion with a complement in Spanish; Jack forced an uncomfortable "Gracias" back at him. After class when the rest of the school was arriving, he stayed inside to record weekend English essays.

"How was basketball?"Mr. Martinez asked. "First game's tomorrow."

Jack rose an inch off his chair to rub the seat of his pants.

"Splinter time,"he said. The sound of the first bell

surprised them. He'd need his usual miracle to get by Chambers.

The rush of bodies had settled by the time he reached his locker. The early morning ground was cool and moist. Birds flooded out of the trees, eyeing worms unseen in dewy grass. The last bell subsided into stillness.

Jack was expert at slipping into the back row not being noticed. He just waited until the teacher's head was turned and, preferably, stuck in her purse. The big worry was the minor fuss Annie and Tara made. Ms. Chambers wouldn't catch on by herself.

This Monday he had nothing to worry about. The teacher was almost asleep in her purse. Annie and Tara didn't react at his entrance. They didn't even turn around. Nobody turned around. Maybe it was lack of a challenge, but it seemed almost a let down.

Even practice wasn't fun. Sijohn paced on the sidelines like a caged cat viewing possible pray. Whether it was the coaches yelling or the violence on Friday, practice quickly turned bloody.

To stop a fast break, Eric wrenched his shoulder up into Jamal. The second stringer was loosened from the ball and a tooth. The two players had to be restrained before they damaged each other. Jamal was a fighter: he takes on anybody, starter or not. Jack admired his feistiness but not the orthodontic wobble.

No picnic under the boards, either. Some fire had gone out of the second team. Jack was pushed in jostled like a marble manipulated by pinball Wizard's. Jared and Ryan hit jackpots as they bounce Jack between them.

The second string fell back. Dan McGee finally just put the cards away as the first team ran away and hid. The whistle ending practice was a mercy.

Sijohn took a slow-as-molasses survey of the boys. As always, his suit was perfectly in place. He touched on his vest, looked away, then brought his eyes back. "You boys might... just might... be ready for tomorrow."

Somebody let out a soft whoop. Faint praise was all they got from Sijohn. The team charged for the lockers. Jared took the opportunity to lead another cheer.

"Who we going to beat?" "Oxnard!"

"Who we gonna beat?"

"Oxnard!"came the answer.

"Who?"The question flew again.

"Oxnard"

"I can't hear you!""Oxnard"

The word crescendo through the shower walls right into Sijohn's office. He smiled. The general has the troops ready for war.

The boys trickled out at the gym singing the song battle. Jack marched resolutely past the picnic table, but Jamal corralled him. Against his will, Jack was dragged over to the jock's table again.

Beside the starters, just Jamal and Jack were near the table. Not sitting on it just standing near it.

Warm-up games had elevated them among second stringers. Not equal status, but in the neighborhood. Snatches of basketball talk washed by. "Oxnard is big... I hear they are fierce."

"Gotta rebound..."

"Block off the boards..."

"Who's their best player?"

"Colonna..."

"He's a real jock"

"Yeah..."

Jack shifted from foot to foot. Feeling like not part of the group made him self-conscious. He needed to vindicate himself and become a real member of the group. Then the girls came, erasing all other topics. The cheerleaders poured down the table like sticky honey, clinging to individual boys. Jared and Grace. Jamal and Tara. Jack had... Nobody.

CHAPTER 8

OH, ANNIE WAS there, all right. But she wasn't stuck to her friend Tara like before – – they would've brought her too close. She certainly didn't step forward. Jack finally spotted her standing next to Grace. Both of them were talking to Jared.

With Jamal secure somewhere in Tara's words, Jack tuned to other conversations. Most of them had to do with Saturday's party. Everyone was there, it seemed. The chatter popped in quick burst of energy.

"I hear he asked her out..."

"Well, she's not going."

"Why not? Somebody else ask her?"

"No..."

"No one waits forever"

Jack thought he saw Annie out of the corner of his eye. He turned. She looked at him like he had the plague. While he was thinking about that, the words slacked off right next to him. His friend had run dry of small talk.

Jack felt a touch on his elbow. Jamal was jerking the security blanket. He and Tara were an island of silence in a sea of words. Jack searched his mind for something to say. Then he thought of it.

"Tell Tara about your..." Jack puffed up his cheek.

Jamal nodded....any port in a storm. He folded his lip back. A red-coated incisor barbed out. No reaction from Tara. Jack thought he had said the wrong thing. The lack of response bothered Jamal too.

The small point guard decided a more visual statement was necessary. He dropped the lip to insert a thumb way up into his mouth. Tara glanced helplessly at her friends.

The girls nearby were awestruck. Jamal jiggled the tooth. An experimental giggle floated nervously out of Tara. She listened for validation, for someone to join her.

No one did. Jamal was extreme, too extreme. Tara's face stiffened into a mask of denial. This really wasn't happening. Jamal still didn't get it. The jury was out, and it didn't look good. In disbelief, Tara cried out: "What are you doing!"

Eric heard the cry and faced his sub. Great, Jack thought. Everyone's watching now. The show was about to begin.

Jamal's face had the proud unconscious error of a new parent just before birth. He was desperate after something to show off. The thumb wormed fiercely under his cheek. The final wrench, the offspring was delivered. A long rooted incisor dripped fresh blood down his fingers. He displayed it for an admiration in the cold twilight. Jack thought, just what everybody wants to see.

But Jamal held it out like a trophy, beaming at them with one less tooth. The perforated grin made him a younger and tinier, like a kid minus a baby tooth. Remaining bubbles of conversation popped into deadness. The gummy read void had grossed the picnic table into muteness.

Tara looked more and more like she didn't want to be with this guy. There was a significant silence. Jack would've clocked it in the minutes rather than seconds. The hush was finally broken by Eric, who had been watching in fascination.

"A..l..l r..i..g..h..t!"

He bawled it out in a slow parental pride. The starter flipped both hands down for a slap shake. If Jamal was mother to that birth, Eric was the father. Jamal's grin never wavered. He slapped palms, then surrendered his own for same.

Tara's horror begin to dissolve with that slap. Jamal is being accepted; he was one of the boys. The spanks from the second set of fingers edged her closer to Jamal.

No one edged closer to Jack. Maybe his call in life was to be a security blanket. He left obediently when Jamal touched his elbow again. At the gate he scanned back for Annie, but she wasn't there.

He peddled with all his weight on the way home, standing up on his bicycle. When the farm trail dip downward -- right before Bottoms Up— Jack melted his body into the bike frame.

From that low view, he saw the canyon snap up at him. His head lower between the handlebars, cutting wind resistance.

The ramp seemed to beckon in like a crooked bet, one he couldn't win. Just for an instant he thought of sailing off and gliding into the wind. He remembered the cycle fight, then released from the bonds of earth.

Jack brodied to a stop at the last minute. Dirt tumbled over the ramp, adding another coat of dust to Mark Lowe's bike. Only the caliper brakes had any silver left to catch the light from the setting sun. His mother wasn't there when he arrived home. Jack didn't even stop at the kitchen on the way to his room. He took Annie's invitation from the warm hug of mattress and box spring. The heavy paper was pressed like thin cardboard. He sank down on the bed, flipping the empty promise up in the air. Too late now.

He traced to the meandering black ink that spelled out his name. The white brushstrokes asked who he was, who he'd be. Jack opened the invitation for the hundredth time and for the last time. Love Annie it said. An emptiness retched through his chest. Regret and opportunity missed. Realization and doing nothing was saying no. Anger and fear inside him felt so strong. He was no better than his mother.

He tore the invitation in half, right down the middle. He did it again and again and again until his hands overflowed with little pieces of a dream.

He started to cry, face stepped into a pillow. Convulsions rambled through lungs but no tears came. A deep guttural moan heaved out of his throat like a storm without rain.

The next day brought sunshine and new hope. It was the day of the first game and he was early. In the distance, light shimmer behind the window pain. His bike gave Mr. Martinez' car some company in the lot. Jack poked his head into the warm room.

"Buenos Dias, Senor Marston"

"Our first game's today."Jack ignored the Spanish.

"I make one big game a year. Is this one it?"

"I probably won't even play."Jack was glad at the quick return to good old English.

"Come on,"the teacher coaxed. "I bet you get in and win with a free throw. Look around— I might be there."

The Spanish class that followed seemed longer than usual. The ringing of bells expelled bodies towards first period.

"See you later, Mr. Martinez."

"Adios, mi amigo," was thrown back as he went out the door.

Jack liked the teacher more than he did the class. The second bell rang while he was still walking to class. As usual, Ms. Chambers was bent over her desk shuffling through papers when he arrived.

The quiet slide into his seat was a masterwork that went unappreciated. A crime wasn't a crime if nobody knew about it. He spied at Annie and saw she was in her cheerleading uniform. She didn't look up- times had changed permanently.

Math class itself seemed permanently longer. It

was hard to concentrate on the equations written on the board. His mind drifted to the game. Oxnard had defeated Kennedy in soccer with their tall star player Colonna. All the school will be there for the opener.

In the middle of fifth period, the call came for the basketball team. Jack found the lockers serene compared to the noisy class he had left. The players dressed in a section that had a chalk board for outlining plays. Dan McGee had put a brand-new uniform in each locker. Jack had number 25. No drop of sweat had yet touched the virgin sheen. A glisten of newness mirrored the fluorescent lights above, even off cotton. With playing time unlikely, it was apt to stay new for a long time.

Jack put it on. The navy blue uniform hung loose from coat hanger shoulders. Mr. Sijohn raised his fist and the team circled him. No whistle required today. Jack slouched with the second stringers in the back. The coach's voice remained soft, but it pierced the corners of the room.

"Oxnard whipped us before. That's the past! Don't worry about it. Play the man-to-man defense we practiced. Help each other out if you have to switch. No stars on this team- win it for each other."

The players clapped and kept on clapping. They bolted into a crooked line and snaked out to the floor. The Kennedy students had already encircled the court, obscuring out-of-bounds lines under shuffling feet. Cheerleaders, wind-milling their arms, diffused through the student section.

The column divided at midcourt for lay-up drills.

Jack jumped high as he could, hand brushing net on the way down. Running back, he inspected the cheerleaders at the other end. Annie faced the crowd, her back to him. Jared, the captain, met referees near the stands. The rest of the team broke into a half-circle around the basket. Two players stood under to rebound balls back to shooters. The starters got most of the chances. Jack shot twice, made one. A buzzer sounded. The game was about to begin.

Dereck paired against Colonna at the center jump. Eric was Kennedy's point man, the ball handler. Jared and Moe flanked him on the wings and his covers underneath were Dereck and Ryan.

Even from the bench Jack felt tension as the ball went up. The centers uncoiled, appearing to reach the height of their jump at the same instant. Both missed the even higher toss of the referee. The red shirt pogoed right back up and tapped it safely to Oxnard.

The game was on!

CHAPTER 9

THE OXNARD GUARDS dribbled upcourt without pressure from Kennedy. When they passed the mid-line, the defense clamped down on the ball. Jared and Ryan shut off the advance by playing in front of their men.

Suddenly a forward caught Jared overplaying. A sweaty jersey streaked for the hoop. Colonna shoveled a behind-the-back pass. Even as players gathered to crash the boards, Jack knew it was too easy to miss. The ball whistled through the net.

Sijohn stepped in front of the bench, two fingers up. Oxnard faded into a tightly packed zone. Eric dribbled to the center of the floor and repeated the two finger salute. Without delay he tossed Moe in the far corner, as Jack knew he would. Moe bounced the ball to Ryan at the base line. Jared started his cut through the middle.

Colonna figured the play out and braced himself in the key. It looked like Jared had room to dodge the center, but instead he blasted right through him. They both went down in a jumble.

A striped shirt hovered over the fallen players like a puzzled traffic cop. The collision was somebody's fault. A decision had to be made without anybody seeing hesitation. The ref droned out:

"Foul on blue..."

Jared looked at his shirt in disbelief. That was his color. The voice droned again "Number 22..."

Jared looked closer. That was his number. He was astonished. His mouth creased into anger, the anger into rage. He jumped into the ref's face.

"He stepped right in front of me."The protest blared all the way to the stands. The official's voice belted right back:

"Red team had position."Then out of the side of his mouth, for only Jared had to hear: "Any more comments and you're looking at a 'T.'"

Jared kept muttering, but gave Dereck his spot for the freethrow. The captain stalked a serpentine route downcourt, almost brushing into the ref.

He couldn't resist it. Jared leaned in to say one last word, Instantly the striped shirt wheeled away from him. It was a nasty word. Facing the scorer's table, the zebra howled for the crowd to hear:

"Technical foul!"

His voice was not as loud as Jared's. The captain spewed out abuse. Finally Sijohn unfolded his arms. He glanced down the bench at Jack. Jared saw it and let himself be waved down the floor with the rest of the team.

No one from either side was allowed along the lanes. Annie, Grace and Tara held their hands at their sides. The crowd needed no agitating. The raucous fans backed up Jared anyway. He had suffered an injustice. It was a home game, after all.

Number nineteen for Oxnard set up for the free-throw. He cradled the ball in one hand, massaged it with the other, then straight-armed it through the net. The crowd hushed, cold water flung in the face.

The cheerleaders cranked into the motion again. The gym rocked full volume when the clock started...
"Get that ball."

"Get that ball."

"Get that ball."

The home team was bent on satisfying the student body. An Oxnard guard forced a pass inside and Ryan poked it away. Eric won the race for the loose ball. Before the offense could change to defense, Jared bolted out front.

In answer to his wave, Eric lofted a high floater. Jared seized it, dribbled it, and launched it off the backboard. The crowd whooped as it swished the net.

Kennedy jammed fastbreak after fastbreak down the throat of Oxnard. Colonna attempted to lead a minor comeback, but the big team lacked speed to run up and down the floor. It was a race.

The bench cleared in the second half and so did half the stands. Empty seats pocked the gym. It was all anti-climactic now. Energy slowly drained out of the cheers. The scoreboard showed the home team securely ahead by sixteen points, Jack stared at the referee. The ref gazed back with eyes open but blind. No clock stopping fouls would delay this fiasco.

The second stringers handled the ball like a hot potato. They expected to watch this game, not pass and dribble in front of an audience...a home audience at that. Jack snagged two rebounds, but both times it was turned back over.

The guards controlled the game, never sifting the ball down to the front line. Perspiration was itching Jack's scalp when Jamal held up two fingers. It was the same play that clotheslined Jared. Colonna saw it too.

Jack waited for the ball to go to the opposite corner, then low to the baseline. Colonna ignored his feint to the right. Jack had to follow the play anyway. When he cut down the middle, Jamal tossed a perfect bounce-pass.

Colonna let him get as far as the key. A forearm jolted into a short uppercut. Jack bounced off the big man's elbow and hit the deck like a squashed bug. He wasn't hurt bad, but stayed down.

A blind ref could call this by braille. Reluctantly, whistles sang a simultaneous sweet song. Jack snapped to his feet even before the whistling stopped. He was after freethrows, not trouble.

Sijohn hurled a scream of inarticulate rage at Colonna. It almost woke the crowd up, what was left of them. It seemed out of place from the Kennedy bench. The game was a laugher. Even Jack wasn't angry at the hit he'd taken.

He stepped to the line for a shot nobody cared

about. He centered the basket in his crosshairs, then shattered the net. Jack bagged his first point of the season. Only he cared.

The refs put the ball back into play, swallowing their whistles for the duration. Only felonious assault would get another foul called. Everyone but Jack was happy when the horn sounded. It was the end of bogus stardom and back to understudy.

The lockers teemed with high spirits. While Dereck was in the shower, Jared hid the center's street clothes. The big man finally dug through the dirty laundry chute. In disgust, he held the clammy garments in front of his nose. Dereck refused to laugh, which made it funnier. Jack felt in a unique position to enjoy laundry jokes.

Jared and Eric twisted their towels into weapons, snapping the wet ends at naked bodies. When Sijohn barged through the door, they froze before he saw what was happening. The coach had low tolerance for horseplay. He raised his fist. There was quiet.

"Good game," the coach pronounced. "I'm proud of you." He gave his customary tug on the vest. "Hard work paid off." A ripple of self-congratulation ran through the room. The coach let the wave run its course.

"Today's just a start. Don't get big heads over the first game. But if they're all like this... I'll be satisfied."

There was general hoopla after the last sentence. In a few minutes the wet headed boys streamed outside to their friends. Jamal went off to try a solo with Tara sans security blanket. Annie and Grace meandered away with a group of slow walking starters. Jack was alone.

He straddled his bike and pushed for the farm trail. He was at Bottoms Up before he knew it and skidded to a stop. While tiptoeing around the ditch, he imagined himself stealing the ball. He'd soar to the sky for a breakaway dunk. Swish a freethrow with a second left. They'd go crazy.

The crowd...

The cheerleaders...

Annie...

His mother'd be there, even his brother.

Maybe it'd be the one game for Mr. Martinez.

A stumble on a wet pebble roused him with a splash to reality. There was dirt again, instead of hardwood, crumbling beneath his shoes.

It'll never happen, Jack thought. He kicked the pebble into the earth.

CHAPTER 10

EVEN IF HE hadn't played much, the game was something for Jack to dream on. The atmosphere seeped into his brain, supplying a structure for the repetitions of practice.

But school dragged. On Tuesday, Mrs. Chambers tried "jigsawing"again in math. Jack's group didn't reunite with Annie's. From the corner of the room, he watched her anyway.

She caught him looking. He didn't turn away. She didn't either. She was as still and cold as a sculpture in ice. Her eyes glittered at him like gems encased in an iceberg.

His neck shivered. A breeze out of the north pole ran down it, made a "T"at his shoulder, dropped down his spine. Cold light from her eyes glimmered, distorted by layers of ice.

When school let out, he ran for the gym. Most of the student body hurried in the reverse direction. Jack thought, playing a sport beat going home at 3 PM.

Ryan and Dereck were shooting by the time Jack arrived.

Gradually, the rest of the team strolled out to join them. It became harder and harder to rebound. Jack was glad when Sijohn started the drills. Better to wait in line for a turn than to kill for the ball. He paired up to shoot twenty-five freethrows.

Jamal went under to rebound the ball back to the line. Rebound wasn't exactly the right word- Jack's twenty-five went in. He didn't bother to dribble- that would upset the rhythm. It was rapid-fire time.

Bang...

Bang...

Bang...

After the first ten, Jamal got under the hoop and used his fist to punch it back out. It caught Sijohn's attention, although his face betrayed no emotion. After layups, the coach explained how to defend a full-court press.

Jack was positioned as center-man at midcourt in a two-on-two. The second team played dummies for a while as the starters walked through it. Then the scrimmage started to see if it would work.

First time down Jamal shot through the press like a shotgun pellet. He skidded to a halt at the top of key and shoveled a pass to Jack. A head fake left Jared airborne; the underhand bucket was anticlimactic.

Second time down was a repeat, except Jack pulled back for a jumper. Dan's cards showed the same result; two points. The press forced the pace, emphasizing speed over rebounding.

The trouble was, the second string was winning. At first, Sijohn interrupted to explain each breakdown to the starters. By the middle of practice, he was shouting not explaining. The starters couldn't stop the second string combo. Jamal dribbled the ball and Jack put it in the basket.

Eric and Jared tried to rattle the short guard by collapsing on him. At first, Jamal couldn't see over their heads. But the defenders were undermanned if the little sub could get rid of the ball.

Jamal solved the problem with a high hook pass. He tossed it over his head, semi-blind, where he figured Jack could be. He figured right. Jack had drifted by instinct to the open area. He gobbled in the pass gratefully and scored again.

They were a team. Jamal doled out the assists; Jack spun them into easy baskets. Together they added a new element to Kennedy- a speed dimension that left the ex-soccer players panting. Jamal was too short to ever be a great basketball player and Jack lacked confidence but together the press and Fastbreak showcased their skills.

Sijohn was not happy. This time it was the first string grateful for the whistle ending practice. The starters had to remain circled on the floor listening to a lecture. The Kennedy second string was not nearly as good as Vista's first string would be.

For the first time, Jack's team had accumulated more of Dan McGee's cards. As a reward, they went home early. The starters still surrounded Sijohn when

Jack left the lockers. Kennedy would be in bad shape against Vista if they couldn't beat their own second team.

The electric blue motorcycle was in the driveway when Jack arrived home. It figured. This was his mother's long night at the hospital. Jack dropped his coat on the floor on the way to the bedroom.

Grant was slouched in the easy chair watching TV. His pants and shirt sheened in black leather. It was protection from street rash if he took a spill. But it also looked cool. Jack said:

"How long you here for?"

Grant turned lazily. "What do you care?"

"Mom works late tonight."

"So?"

"She wants to see you."

Grant went back to the television set. Jack turned to leave his bedroom.

"Wait," Grant said. From the other side of the chair he picked up something. He tossed it at little brother. The laundry bag jarred Jack back a step. Grant said without question mark;

"How about a rush job."

"Come home on a weekend."

Grant's eyes strayed from the TV.

Jack gave the laundry a rough kick. It rolled over once. He said softly:

"No."

Grant's dark eyes slithered up his brother's shirt. He hissed:

"What did you say?" Jack said it again.

Grant raised up, like it pained him. He turned the television off.

Jack backed out of the room. He kept backing up until he tripped on his coat. He put it on and kept going until he was on his bike.

He pedaled hard until he reached the farm trail. There he stopped and coasted down the slope. Bottoms Up stopped his advance. He gazed down and thought of all the times he'd said yes, all the times he'd sat on coattails and enjoyed the ride. He couldn't remember the last time he said no to Grant.

Thunder crackled faintly in the twilight canyon.

Jack listened.

The rumble intensified.

It was a 250 cc engine.

It was getting closer.

CHAPTER 11

IT WAS SEMI-DARK, colors fading, when Grant pulled up. The electric blue gas tank was now just ordinary blue. The black leather almost disappeared in the nightshade. His brother's face, disembodied, looked curious over chrome handlebars. A helmet topped the backrest like a forgotten piece of armor. The stand was kicked down, the engine turned off, but Grant didn't dismount.

"Thought I'd find you here."

Jack rolled his bike back a couple of feet. His bicycle seemed inadequate. The massive motorcycle made him feel like a little boy playing in a sandbox.

"I've got something for you." Grant turned towards the back of his bike. The laundry sack was roped behind him.

Jack backed up another half wheel turn. He thought of his mother for some reason. She'd be coming home at midnight.

"Stay and see Mom and I'll do it."

"What do you care?" His brother spat in the dirt.

Jack knew why, but couldn't think of how to say it.

Grant moistened the dust at his feet again. He turned the key and the motor boomed to life.

"I don't understand,"Grant said. "I gotta go back to school."

Jack focused beneath his brother's face, where leather jacket closed on collarbone. He didn't answer.

"Are you going to do it or not?"

"No." Jack rolled back farther, away from the ditch. He was almost in the bushes now.

The throttle aroused the engines into a furious howl. Grant let the clutch out and moved off. A couple of hundred yards away, he stopped. Jack couldn't see his face, couldn't read what was in it.

The shadow figure turned, unlatched the helmet from the backrest. He tugged it on, snapped the strap across chin. The fingers twisted the right grip.

The cylinders caterwauled. The front wheel leapt up and stayed up. The nothingness of bottoms up loomed ahead. His brother was going for it, going for it in the dark.

The engine pitched higher, higher. Jack backed unconsciously into the underbrush. Grant could change his mind. He could go for the skinny neck of the gorge, or even around it altogether.

But that would be backing down, admitting he couldn't make it. And, of course, he had done it before. But that was before sunset. How could Grant make it if he couldn't see the ramp? With headlight switched off, the silhouette shot through the dim horizon.

Jack glanced away to line up the ramp. It was hard to see it in the dark, even as close as he was. Grant must have been searching for it, too. The head lamp switched on when he was fifty yards away. A rope of rigid light probed the abyss like the white cane of a blind man.

It was then that Jack knew there was trouble. The cycle was off line. Jack's angle was enough to see that. Grant might miss the ramp, or not hit it flush. Jack shouted:

"Go around it!"

He might as well have been talking to himself. Veering away would have been chickening out. The thundering bike dipped into a turn, correcting in a diagonal line for the wide bottom of Bottoms Up. The rocketing machine hit the ramp square in the center, but the off line approach flew Grant sideways over the canyon. The cycle twisted and flattened out, like a table-top. The headlamp's strip of light lasered across the divide like misdirected fireworks.

No audience cheered the aerobatics. Just a little brother gaping into bad light. Jack knew what it was like. His eyes might have been closed, but he had wafted through the sky.

Jack couldn't see it but heard the back tire bust against dirt. Even sideways, even in blackness, Grant had made it. His brother had corrected the twisting bike in midair.

The rider brodied to a stop to savor his conquest.

He didn't wave, just froze for a moment in silent statement. Leathered black knight on faded blue charger, half-vanished in a lost sunset.

The engine yowled, the wheel leapt up again, the figure faded from view. The groan of the engine moaned down to silence. Jack and his unmotorized transportation came out of the bushes.

The spectacle of the jump was over, another memento of glory. Excitement was Grant's legacy, and power. The younger brother began the laborious roll up the hill home.

CHAPTER 12

HE THOUGHT ABOUT telling his mother about Grant's visit. He didn't know if she'd be happy he came or sad he left without seeing her. Jack had a feeling the show had been for little brother alone. He didn't tell her.

She surprised him by coming home in time for dinner the next day. The kick on the screen door told Jack her mood. He waited in his bedroom for the clatter to fade. When the banging of pan against pan subsided, he stuck his nose in the kitchen.

His mother sat behind a bottle of cold white wine. Hot chili was on the stove. He removed the pan from the fire and slid the lid back. Beneath escaping steam bubbled the brown main course. His nostrils filled with the aroma. He sank across from her.

"Broomhead let you out early."

"She didn't let me out anywhere."

She took a drink from the glass. Jack watched her

do it. Her chin was out, defiant. Her mouth was sad.

"I'm over 21. I finished my work and I left."

"What about Broomhead's work?"

No answer on that. Jack decided it was a good time to get chili. He decorated two bowls with saltine crackers, then ladled the beans into equal portions. And water for himself—lots of water. His mother had chopped a bowl of onions, and he scattered them over the top. Chili was no good without onions.

He dug in. His dining partner poured out a second drink. He caught her eyes beneath the stem of the glass. Sadness seemed to have won out over defiance. Jack made a try at comfort. When his cheeks had receded to half full he said:

"This isn't the only hospital in town."

"I told you I'm used to Memorial." She pushed the drink back and the bowl forward. She took a dainty stab of food, whispering into the bowl:

"If old Broomhead would leave...,"

"And I told you that's probably not going to happen, Mom,"

He loved his mother and wanted her to be realistic. In this sense, they were good for each other. They were a family, they had each others back. Of course he didn't have to confront Broomhead. Jack liked giving advice more than taking it.

"Applied for Head Nurse yet?"

"Head Floor Nurse," his mother corrected. Her spoon dropped into the chili with a thick brown splash.

She pushed the bowl back as if that answered the question. Jack waited. She said:

"I've had enough."

Jack waited some more. She knew what he asked. Finally she gave in and answered.

"Deadline's not for weeks."She picked up her glass again and loaded it. "I'm not ambitious, Jack."

"You're not happy, either."

"Pay's not much better, considering the responsibility."

"That's not the idea. Your boss is a bitch."

"Jack!" His mother was shocked. Whatever Broomhead was, her son wasn't allowed to say it.

"Witch,"he corrected. "I said witch."

"I know what you said, all right, young man."

She took a long drink, almost draining it. She left a little on purpose—it wasn't ladylike to gulp. A long gray fog clouded her eyes. The conversation was over. They left the dishes in hot water to soak the night.

School was the usual stuff, but warm-ups at practice brought a surprise. During layups, his name was called from the bench. It was Dan McGee, just come in from somewhere. Out of breath, his face was red as his freckles.

"Marston!" He yelled again. Jack was next in line to shoot, but gave up his place.

"What's up, Dan," he said, feeling faintly like Bugs Bunny.

"Coach wants you in the office."

"What about?" Calls like that were trouble.

"Ask him,"said Dan. "I'd go pronto. "

"Ok,"Jack said, but he didn't run. Trips to the office—even to a coach's office—made him nervous. Could he be cut at this late date? What needed to be said in private?

The door was open when he arrived. The coach, dressed in usual formality, hunched over the desk. His oversized chair smelled like real leather. It looked like it belonged in a lawyer's office instead of a gym. The chair's size and opulence were meant to impress.

Jack waited for a moment, wasn't noticed, finally rapped on the door frame. Sijohn said without looking up:

"Come in."

A stubby hand waved toward a bare-bones chair of wood and nails. Jack took it, hard frame rubbing cold against his tank top. The coach's eyes seemed to sink in their sockets like a tired sunset. He took a pencil between his fingers and tapped the eraser on the wood.

"I've been watching you."

His voice was smooth and soft, unlike the bellicosity of practice. Nevertheless, Jack's spine went straight against the hard-backed chair.

Sijohn perceived the tension. He stuck the pencil in his top vest pocket and rolled back slightly in the chair. A heavy breath faintly whistled through the front teeth. Jack sat even straighter n the wooden chair. The coach said:

"You've got quickness."

Jack tilted his head as if to improve comprehension.

"I like that in a forward,"the coach said. "I think you can make a difference for the team. Especially if you get help on the big guys."

"I can?"

"Don't you think you can?"

"I never thought about it."

Player and coach knew it was a lie. Every second stringer thinks about it, if dreams count. Sijohn squeezed his eyelids together.

"You don't belong here unless you want to be first string."

Jack slouched forward, relaxing a bit. This news wasn't bad, just unexpected. Astonished, he said:

"I've never started at anything."

Didn't say you'd start,"the coach grumped. "You earn that. Doesn't matter who starts, anyways. Matters who finishes. And when it's over, matters who won the game. Point is, you can do more than mop-up."

Sijohn waited for Jack to speak up. When he couldn't wait anymore he said:

"You're gonna get some minutes."

Jack's face didn't change, just stayed blank and open.

"Think you belong out there?"

Jack hesitated, uncertain.

"Well?"The coach's eyes widened for the first time.

"Yessir,"Jack spit out. It was all he could think to

say.

Sijohn dismissed him. Jack bumped the wood chair over on the way out of the office. He picked it up without looking back.

The coach removed the pencil from his vest. He tapped a staccato message on the desk. Rolling back in his chair, he bit into the eraser. The soft grip of the leather cushions enveloped the body. His eyes rolled back into the sunset.

CHAPTER 13

FAINT EXCITEMENT TINGLED in the morning sunshine: Jack always liked the feeling of game day. The special tension accelerated his morning ride to school. He was anxious already for the game to start.

Usual daydreams kept him company. What would the other school's court look like? He pictured himself catching a pass from Jamal ahead of the chasing pack. He would hush the Vista crowd with a driving lay in.

As he approached the grey block building, excitement bubbled in his chest. Jack has already poked his head into room 212 when he remembered his bike was unlocked. He greeted his teacher, who was busy chalking Spanish phrases onto the board.

"What's new, Jack?"

English today, Jack thought with gratitude. Mr. Martinez stopped writing. Jack stood in the doorway, heat escaping into the frosty morning.

"... a game today."

"Good luck in it!"

"Can't mess up sittin' on the bench." He let go of the door. It glided toward him with the hiss of air pressure. Martinez's answer slipped around the edge before it shut.

Jack scrambled to his bike thinking about that. "Give it your best shot," the teacher said.

"Best shot to do what?" Jack thought. "To cheer the other ones?"

At one o'clock the basketball squad was excused to board the bus. It was the first ride for the team together. The driver was a middle-aged, skinny woman named Mrs. Dodd. As the boys loaded, she half hid in the bushes to smoke a cigarette.

The starters pushed and shoved to claim their seats in the back of the bus – the divine right of the first stringers everywhere. When everyone was aboard, Mrs. Dodd sucked in a last drag. She snuffed the butt and got behind the wheel.

When Jared pushed Eric over a seat, the driver's face popped into the rearview mirror. She looked vaguely unhappy. The vagueness left when Eric retaliated with a shove of his own. The driver slammed clipboard against gearshift knob. Just the first two rows noticed her displeasure. She got up.

Mrs. Dodd stepped down the aisle in her best intimidation walk. It half worked. A hush followed in in her wake. Only the boys in the back didn't give her the courtesy of quiet. For them, you had to earn it. She tried to get their attention.

"My name's Mrs. Dodd..."That announcement did nothing. In sterner tone she said:

"Stop acting like children!"

Still no reaction. Her voice dropped into the "I'm not kidding"range of threat.

"... or would you rather your coach come back here?"

The first-stringers settled down at the magic word, "coach."They didn't need Sijohn upset at them. His disposition was prickly enough without encouragement from a bus driver.

An undertone of grumblings rippled beneath the peace. Even that soon disappeared. The team dropped from silence to somberness by the time Vista came into view.

The gym was modern enough from outside, but inside it looked like a relic from long ago. Dance decorations dangled from coffee-brown rafters like souvenirs from an ancient, old dance. Kennedy was assigned the girls' locker room as a dressing room.

Each player had an individual cubicle designed for extra privacy. Pulling down his tank top, Jack felt butterflies in his stomach flutter. He thought unhappily of chili and onions. He pounded up the stairs and out to the hardwood floor.

The stands were shrouded in orange. The uniformity even included the paint on the dance banners overhead. The hometown fans, also in orange, hissed as the visitors took the court. The banners themselves seemed to join in, wrinkling overhead without benefit of wind.

The few Kennedy fans huddled together. Annie Tara, and Grace pinwheeled their arms in desperate rotations. No matter what they did, the cheerleaders couldn't stir them up. The cheers were swallowed by overwhelming decibels from the Vista rooting section. Finally, the girls dropped their hands in futility. They turned tail on the non-fans to watch their team warm-up.

The physical exertion of the layups seemed to wake up the players. The starters chirped encouragement to each other. Jared, as captain, made the required visit to the scorer's table. With the game about to begin, Jack found his usual place on the bench. He had to discuss the finer points of battle with Jamal.

First thing they noticed was Vista's size. This was reinforced when the teams walked out for the tip and stood next to each other. Three were bigger than Dereck. Dereck stretched high on the jump ball, but the orange center tapped it first. Jack turned to Jamal.

"You can't beat height."

Number thirty-one dribbled down the baseline. He put a quick fake on Jared and let loose a jumper. The ball ricocheted off the base of the rim. Eric timed his leap perfectly. The guard tossed it out to Jared, then circled for a pass-back. Before Eric reached him, an orange shirt barreled into the screen.

The whistles were automatic. Jared was tangled on the floor—this was getting to be a habit. The gold chain with the razor blade had bounced out of his jersey, flapping against his chest. The blocky captain corkscrewed to his feet. Thirty-one, still wobbly, started to get up, too. Jared gave him a little shove in the back.

Thirty-one grabbed at Jared's jersey in order to keep his feet. He hooked into the captain's jewelry instead, and used it to pull himself upright. Jared's neck jackknifed down, but it was thirty-one who screamed.

Jack heard it from the bench. The hand that grabbed the necklace was painted across with a stripe of red blood. The zebras intervened before anything else happened. Since neither official had seen who started it, technical were called on both players.

Thirty-one complained, but retired to his bench to have his hand examined. After a delay, he was called back out to shoot the "T." The home coach wouldn't let him go, still tending the hand. The refs grew impatient to get the game moving.

Finally, they suggested another player shoot the technical. The team's best foul shooter could enter the game just to sink it. Vista's problem was that thirty-one was their best man at the line. The coach must have calculated that. He whispered something to his injured star.

The gym clapped for the hero's return. Thirty-one's walk back to the court was slow, but he was quick enough to sink his "T". The roar that followed the ball through the hoop didn't let up. The refs waved everyone away for the other half of the double technical. This one was not as popular.

Jared was in a "better hold me back"mode, snarling away at anything orange He cooled down the act when it came time to shoot, but Sijohn wasn't looking at him. Instead, he pointed to the end of the bench.

"Twenty-five,"the coach said.

Nobody moved. Nobody knew who it was. Jamal took a closer look at Jack's jersey, realized it was twenty five, then gave his pal a "wake me up"slap on the head.

Jack, suddenly aware of perspiration under his uniform, unglued himself from the bench. His trunks unpeeled from the wood like skin off an old sunburn.

"Just like practice." Sijohn said.

Jack made the short trip to the scorer's table, then passed by the bench again. The coach gave him a pat on the sticky trunks. Jamal's voice shrilled out:

"Can it for us, buddy!"

The rebounders were shooed back behind Jack's line of vision. Unfortunately, the referees did not supply earplugs. A blitzkrieg of noise assaulted his ears. Jack looked at the hoop, then through the glass backboard. Orange towels undulated up and down as if a soft breeze might blow the skinny sub away.

It was enough to unnerve a veteran, much less a rookie whose main skill was warming benches. The referee tried to say something, but couldn't be heard. He improvised by pointing one index finger down—single shot coming. The basketball was spun into Jack's hands.

His fingertips scuffed over the leather. Oddly enough, the texture of the ball lessened his fear. This was something he knew how to do. His nails scraped against the leather again for reassurance. The massage soothed his nerves. He had done this a thousand times, a million times.

Jack tunneled his vision into a pinprick on the back of the rim. The wind storming towels went into hurricane season. He bounced the ball once, twice. Right arm straightened, wrist snapped. The free throw swished. Orange towels wrinkled back onto their owners.

He pushed himself off the stage. He was back on the bench again. Jared and the rest of the five circled around Sijohn. They didn't notice Jack walk by. He absorbed Jamal's slap on the rear, then sank down on the end of the bench.

The Vista coach scrutinized the visitors when they took the floor. Jared, still scowling, tramped out to the forward spot. The yellow metal was hidden, tucked away under his jersey instead of flapping out like a weapon. The referee was flagged down anyway. The coach's words were indistinct to the fans but audible to the Kennedy bench.

"Get that damn thing off him!"

He slashed a forefinger across his palm to indicate the injury. The pantomime clued in the crowd. They booed lustily. The referee enforced the will of the majority. The necklace was ordered off.

Jared gave ref and coach consecutive dirty looks, but did as commanded. His reluctance brought a rain of boos down on him. He stalked back to his spot like a man wronged.

The ruckus seemed to ignite the home team. Their tall front line could play Jared's way—a game of laying body-on-body. Missed shots were followed to the hoop by heaving flesh. Second, third, even fourth efforts were tapped back to the rim.

The Vista audience howled like a congress of banshees. Dance banners waved over the proceedings in bold splendor, as if fanned by the madness. Vista wedged out a short lead by controlling the boards.

At the eye of the storm, the Kennedy fans sat on their hands, oblivious to cheerleader pleas. There wasn't anything to cheer about. When the half ended, Kennedy was lucky to trail by seven. It was still a game, but barely, and it wouldn't be much longer.

During halftime, Sijohn didn't make any impassioned speeches. The starters spent the time practicing shots at the new basket. Dan told Jamal and Jack to join them. Jamal wondered about it but Jack suspected.

The preliminary buzzer sounded for the second half. Sijohn pointed to the scorer's table. Jamal was in for Eric, Jack for Jared.

This wasn't garbage time. Kennedy still had a chance. Jack stepped out onto the hardwood. There was feeling of fear yet excitement at the prospect of being in the game and perhaps making a difference for the team.

CHAPTER 14

THE NEWCOMERS JOINED the sweat-stained starters in the huddle. Seven players, instead of five, ran a circle around Sijohn. The coach noticed the surplus numbers around him. He tapped two veterans.

Eric got the message and took Jamal's seat on the bench. Jared gave Jack the same look he had given thirty-one. Instead of taking a seat, he paced down to the water cooler. Sijohn said to the second half starters:

"Vista's killing us on the boards. Only way to beat them is to run them." He draped arms around two fresh jerseys. "Jamal and Jack'll get us off the blocks.

The ref whistled for the jump. The Vista crowd ballyhooed their team out. They expected a full-fledged rout in the second half. The Kennedy fans were passive—you had to be philosophical in a massacre. Jack stepped next to thirty-one, Jared's man.

The zebra dipped the ball, then popped it between the centers. The orange jersey slapped it cleanly, but Jamal snaked in front to steal it. Dribbling with his right hand, he called a play with the left.

The pass sailed to Ryan. Dereck circled off the high post and skidded to a stop. Jack faked inside, then shifted outside Dereck's hip. The defender flicked away like cigar ash. Ryan kicked the ball inside and Jack swooped it to the backboard. The ball twirled from glass to twine.

Jack pointed to Ryan as he raced back—-the crowd should know who made the assist. Ryan's fist flung into the air. It made Jack feel he belonged. He'd shot the "T"all alone, court cleared off. Now he was in a five man game. The Kennedy people put together a few claps.

On defense, Jack lagged a step in back of his man. He seemed preoccupied with his own glory at having scored a basket. Thirty-one waved wildly for the ball. Jack jerked forward as the pass came airborne. His hand knifed in to slash it away.

Jamal pounced on the loose ball and charged the other way. Jack blazed up on the right. Ryan filled the left lane. Jamal halted his dribble at the free throw line. He looked both ways, only slightly moving his head.

Ryan slanted from the left; Jack poured in from the right. The pass bounced left. Ryan floated up an overhand shot but the ball rolled right over the rim. Jack snagged the rebound with two hands and popped it back to the glass. This time the ball settled in nicely.

Annie, Grace and Tara rolled in cartwheels as Jack sank back. The crowd in front of them stirred in restless waves. This was the game they came to see. Kennedy was three points from the home team.

The Vista coach signaled for a timeout. Momentum

was switching. Even the crowd could feel it. Dance banners hung limp overhead, as if only lung power had ruffled them before.

The pleas of the Kennedy cheerleaders were finally answered. The Kennedy fans rose in a small ovation: a noisy blue island in a silent orange sea. Jack felt part of it.

The fourth quarter was not even close. Kennedy's fast break had never worked like this, even in practice. Before the buzzer sounded, Jack had three more baskets...on assists from Jamal...and notched another free throw.

Energy ran like an electric current through the locker room. The building quieted a little...not much.. when Sijohn entered. He was smiling, but not dancing around like some of the players. Everyone circled in front of their cubicles. When the hum kept going he said:

"Calm down now. We won a game, not a championship." He waited a few seconds. The joshing subsided.

"Get it out of your system. You've got a long bus ride."

The team disappeared into cubicles, the isolation putting a cork in the celebration. But the boys bubbled again when they met at the bus. Jack climbed in the front with Jamal. The first stringers clamored into the back. Once more, they had the pleasure of Mrs. Dodd.

Jack saw her spying through the mirror when claps resounded from the rear. Her face was joyless as a prison guard's. The slamming palms of her prisoners merged into a pattern. A chant was born in the gap between two thunderous claps.

"We are...number one!"

"We are ...number one!"

"We are ...number one!"

Mrs. Dodd, face tight, bobbed into the rear view mirror again. Jack turned back to see what she was watching. It was Jared, strutting down the aisle like a rooster. He bellowed:

"Who's number one?"

"Kennedy!"Came the salvo.

The vehicle slowed down, then stopped. Jack swiveled back to the front to see why. Iron rails lay ahead. A silly rule made them stop the motor before crossing a railroad track. The front of the bus including Jack continued to cheer.

"Kennedy!"

"Kennedy!"

"Kennedy!"

Jared used the aisle like a stage. He hunched to his knees like a cheerleader and then rocketed up with arms spread. He jumped so high his head bounced off the tin ceiling. In his enthusiasm, he had miscalculated. Jared rubbed the bump on his head comically. The laughter became hysterical.

The motor clicked off. The blare seemed to double in volume. The tumult crescendoed off sheet metal walls without competition from the engine. In the mirror, the jaw of Mrs. Dodd went iron-tight.

"That's enough!"

No response came.

She said it again.

Jack had to lip read her words in the din. Jared, in the back of the bus, was oblivious to the driver. He was squatting in the aisle again, cheerleader like. His hands cupped into a megaphone.

"Who's the best?"

"We are!"Roared the back of the bus.

Mrs. Dodd lurched up from the driver's seat. The subs, reading her fury, closed down the volume as she passed each row. When she reached Jared he was in the middle of a cheer. Her hand reached out and gripped his shoulder like a vice.

"Stop it," she said violently. "Stop it! Act like a human being!"

The sudden pressure startled him. The other starters froze when Jared did. The cacophony vanished like someone had turned off a stereo.

His face blustered out again when he saw it was Mrs. Dodd. She had no power over him. He was still leader of the team. Nothing could change that, especially not a woman bus driver. He shook her hand off. His voice sailed up high to sound like a girl.

"Stop it, stop it!"

It didn't sound like a boy imitating a woman. It sounded strangely real. Mrs. Dodd, taken by surprise, did nothing. She had not expected an imitator. This was a bus not a comedy club.

The team howled in unholy joy. Jared's nerve had

to be rewarded. The faces of the team begged for more. The captain tiptoed up the aisle, hips swaying in feminine exaggeration. His voice went falsetto again, pitch shivering into a woman's vibrato.

"Stop it!"

"Stop...I am Odd Dodd!"

"Odd Dodd!"

"Odd Dodd!"

Mrs. Dodd stood anchored by shock. The bus, still parked by the side of the road, rattled with convulsions out of control. No doubt about it, the boy was good. New voices joined in the driver's ridicule. Insults pelted at her from the back of the bus.

"Sit down, odd Dodd."

"Drive the bus like you are paid to do."

The chant was slow and methodical, as if the bus drivers name was that of a rival. Hot, dark blood flooded Mrs. Dodd's checks. She picked her way back to the front. Her eyes shot out indiscriminate bolts of pain as she passed her tormentors. The cat calls tapered off as Jared also faded into his seat. The boys snickered over Jared's nerve, but not so rowdily. A residue of humor hung on their faces like a dirty joke, one you are ashamed to tell. The bus was even on the quiet side when it rolled into the Kennedy lot.

CHAPTER 15

JACK WAS UP early the next day, but not before his mother. He wanted to tell her about the game, but she had the early shift. Broomhead had used her to plug a vacation hole in the schedule. Jack didn't like it, and said so at breakfast.

"You worked last night. It's not fair to come back the next morning."

His mother sniffed the oatmeal she was stirring.

"Did you apply for Broomhead's job?"

Jack's bowl was full, steam rising like winter's breath. She accompanied the pan back to the stove so she wouldn't have to look at him.

"You didn't do it."

His mother dumped the pan into the sink. "Eat your oatmeal."She ordered.

Jack decided he wasn't hungry. It bothered him when she let people run right over her. He went out the door, cereal still steaming on the table. His mother didn't call him back. He didn't mean to leave this early. The day hadn't really started. He took a short cut through the field.

The earth squished black and rich under his feet, like it could grow anything today. Farm workers were already irrigating lettuce. Even the great ditch appeared less ominous, less deep in the growing light. Mark Lowe's handlebars beckoned at him from the bottom like arms reaching up.

The school was still asleep. Mike, the janitor, burrowed in his heated office like a sleepy mole. Before too long he came out, stretched, and shuffled down the front steps to the flag pole. No flair was required to raise the colors in the early morning. The flag hung limp as Kennedy had left the dance banners of Vista. Perhaps it, too, was waiting for an audience.

A while after that non-ceremony, a blue sedan pulled up. Mr. Martinez stepped out. He balanced a covered cardboard box with one hand and fumbled glasses with the other. Jack waited a decent interval before knocking. He had to tell somebody about the game. The door squeaked open.

The cardboard carton was on the table, lid now popped off. Handwritten essays overflowed in all directions. Half-spectacles tilted off-center on the teacher's nose. That was the penalty for reading too many of them. He took one look at Jack and said:

"You won."

"Better,"Jack said.

Martinez dipped his head to peer over the top of his glasses.

"We won." Jack paused. "And I played." He couldn't stop a smile. "Played when it counted."

The whole story spilled out. Martinez's head bobbed up and down. His eyes winked over the wire frames with "I told you so"pleasure.

Jack described the pressure of the technical, the calming of the flailing towels. How he started the second half, the excitement of the come from behind win.

"You got your chance and hit a bullseye."

"Maybe I'm bragging..."

"Why'd the coach put you in? Why'd he keep you in?" He peered over the granny glasses. "Sijohn's no fool. He knows a winner when he sees one."

Later in the afternoon a girl with long dark braids brought in a little piece of paper. It was green. Students stopped listening. The teacher stopped teaching. Green meant vice principal.

Somebody was in trouble, the rare and popular kind. That is, popular as long as the call slip didn't land on your desk. The girl with the black braids bypassed Jack.

She dropped the green paper in front of Jared, who didn't even waste an extra blink. The captain sniggered at his friends and disappeared out the door with the girl.

Jared was absent when the coach summoned the squad together before practice. Sijohn searched the team room with dark eyes.

"Too bad you had to spoil it,"he said. "You weren't the only ones feeling good yesterday." He stopped, eyes dead.

"Jared has been suspended from the team."

Everyone knew about the call slip, but this was drastic action. Jack's gut told him the whole Mrs. Dodd escapade had been wrong. They had chewed up the bus driver for cheap entertainment.

"How many games?"asked Eric.

"Depends on him." Sijohn looked hard at the first stringers, the ones from the back of the bus. "The bus driver said a lot of you gave her a hard time—Jared was just the leader." He stepped toward the door in disgust.

"I'm disappointed. The woman—Mrs. Dodd—was crying when she told us about it." He turned his back on the team and walked out. When he was out of ear-shot, Eric mumbled:

"That Old Odd Dodd!"

"We ought to fix her,"said Ryan. "She's wrecked our team."

Jack didn't say anything. The faint screech of a whistle ended talk about Mrs. Dodd. The players scattered to the floor. Being late would only make it worse for the rest of them. On the way out, Jamal gave Jack a glance.

"You're in,"he said softly.

CHAPTER 16

IF HE DIDN'T catch Jamal's meaning, Jack soon found out. He was the natural choice for the starting team. Jared's forward spot was his against Edison. The fact it was a home game did nothing to ease his nerves. Everyone would be watching him, judging him. He hadn't earned his way, not yet.

Sijohn had him reverse the practice jersey so that it was right-side out. Gold became blue. Jack tried on his new team like someone wiggling into hand-me-down clothes that didn't quite fit. Squads of both colors looked at him with new eyes. With Jack bumped to the first team, Jamal was left behind to lead the scrubs. "Jack's team"became "Jamal's team,"and they weren't as good.

The surprise of the weekend was that Grant came home on his mother's day off. Mrs. Marston's face lit up for the prodigal son like a Roman candle. She shot around the kitchen preparing the proper fatted calf, even if it was the hamburger variety. Grant reveled in the attention.

During dinner, there were only harmless questions about college. Yes, it made high school seem like kindergarten. No, it wasn't possible to come home any more than he did. And yes, it all made Jack sick. He left the table.

The younger son sank into the easy chair, but the words wafted down the hallway to him. He could picture the rest: his brother's nonchalance, his mother's hero-worshipping eyes. His own eyes fluttered – a combination of too little sleep and too much dinner.

The mention of his name made him conscious. Grant's voice rasped, and Jack's eyelids slit halfway between sleep and surveillance. His mother whispered something.

Why whisper, Jack thought. His ears picked up, rabbit like. After a hushed minute, Grant spoke in a regular voice.

"I don't care if he can hear me or not."He said a little louder, "It's his job to wash the clothes."

Jack hunched forward in the chair, eyes vigilant. His mother's voice was also loud enough to hear.

"He's getting too old to idolize you. He expects you to..."

"Jack doesn't tell me what to do,"Grant interrupted. "Nobody does."A pause emphasized his independence. "You don't either."

Jack strained to hear his mother's reply, but there was nothing. His brother's voice clarioned out again: "I'm a man now."

There was no answer Jack heard. A kitchen chair scraped back. The door slammed. The electric blue dragon started up. When the rumble faded into the night, Jack left the easy chair.

His mother was in the living room, gazing out at the black street from the window. The pane was dark-nothing to see but a reflection of her own face. She turned and looked at her other son without seeing him. The Marston family was down to two again.

Classes were flat as ever on Monday. His thoughts focused on the upcoming Edison game. It was official: Jack was starting. Now his idle dreams weren't so idle. He had a way to make them come true.

But at school even Ms. Chamber's jig-sawing ceased to be interesting. At least the math part of it did. Jack's group, blessed with Mark Lowe was first to finish a piece of the puzzle. Jack volunteered to investigate group two's jigsaw.

Annie happened to be in group two. There was an empty desk next to her. He gently slid into it. She didn't move away, which is the most expected from her. At least he didn't get the frigid look that chilled him inside out.

He bent forward slightly to see over her shoulder. The math problem was partially hidden under long fingernails. Jack tried to peer at it, doing his duty as a student. He slouched closer, into Annie's personal space. She had to notice him.

Her pencil stopped making numbers. She knew who it was by intuition, but he was trespassing. She blinked in his direction, but toward the floor. Jack sucked in a gulp of air. He leaned back, away from her, aware of the rejection.

His chest pushed out the gulp of air. Annie heard the slow breath come out. Her eyes moved from the floor, climbed the body, slowed down, stopped for good waist-high. She also took a swallow of air.

It sounded like a sigh when she released it. A moment went by. Her hand moved off the math paper, exposing it. A shiny fingernail scratched across the jigsaw page. It slid to the top of the desk, under Jack's nose. Easy to see.

But Jack was looking at her, instead.

What else did he want? The eyes of the cheerleader became curious. They ascended Jack's chest, decelerated, finished beneath his chin. They couldn't seem to make it all the way to his face.

She wasn't ready to communicate like that yet. Mark snapped the spell by coming over to talk math. It took the class brain all of two seconds to solve the jigsaw.

Sijohn worked them long and hard at practice. The thumping heat of the shower felt good afterwards. Jack understood how horses slept standing up. Dan threatened to turn the hot water off in order to get him back on dry land. When Jack's head emerged from a towel, he found the locker room empty. Even the manager was gone.

Jack expected the schoolyard to be a ghost town. Instead, the picnic table was graced with the second coming of Jared. He wasn't supposed to be around because of the suspension. But the school was closed now, and everyone had gone home.

The captain wasn't alone; Jared was never alone. Other starters stuck to him like spokes around a hub. Jack clung to the door of the gym and watched. If this was a planned meeting, he had missed the invitation.

It was easy to recognize Dereck, the tallest figure. The center shook his head and separated himself from the group. It was like a bad joke he had been told about somebody's mother. But the others shoved in closer, as if to exchange secrets. The murmurs were indistinct, but no burst of laughter indicated the punchline of a joke.

Then Moe, also easy to identify as the smallest, spotted Jack hugging the building. The point guard alerted the others. The huddle disintegrated. The schoolyard lights sent long shadows with the boys as they dispersed into the darkness. The bench had only a few ants on it when Jack passed it.

CHAPTER 17

THE MIDWEEK GAME against Edison was the next day. Just a few parents were in the audience for the warm-ups. It was an afternoon game, and people had to work. His own mother worked too hard to attend something like this. Mr. Martinez said he'd only attend one big game. For a championship, maybe, he'd be there. Classes at Kennedy were still in sixth period.

The Edison team was already at the other end shooting. Sijohn had warned about a player named Robeson, number nineteen. He led the league in scoring. Jack searched the numbers but couldn't find him. The sweat cooled on his back and Jack gave an involuntary shiver.

The referees tested out two game balls, bouncing them with careful scrutiny. One was selected; the other thrown back. Jack squeezed into his spot around the center circle. The butterflies started churning in his stomach just before tip-off.

Then a bell rang. Almost at once, bodies began to pour into the gym. The trickle of humanity expanded into a steady stream of students. Finally, the refs threw up their hands and left the floor. Annie, Tara, and Grace replaced the zebras on center stage. They began to clap their hands. Soon the whole student section rocked with the beat.

Both teams took advantage of the delay to shoot extra goals. After one try, Jack sat down to let the others warm up. Ryan, Dereck, Eric, and Moe remained on the floor. Jack spotted number nineteen at the other end. Robeson was wide and chunky—like Jared—and sunk hook shot after hook shot.

"Jack,"Sijohn barked. "Get out there and shoot."

He sheepishly joined the others under the basket. He was one of them, at least till Jared got back. When the students were seated, the teams huddled again around their coaches.

"Play together as a team,"Sijohn said to his five. "If they slow it down, it'll be Vista all over again."

Ryan and Eric exchanged glances. They looked at Dereck but the center turned away. Sijohn said:

"Pay attention when I talk!"

The whistle blew and he had to let them go. There was not a lot of noise when Jack walked out with the others. He had imagined students saying, "Where's Jared?" But everyone knew that story by now. He wasn't allowed to come to games or any school function. Jared was too smart to try that. It would mean bigger trouble than now. As Jack wedged around the jumping circle, Ryan abruptly stepped in front.

"I'll take Robeson."

Jack made the switch, a bit surprised. He had handled thirty-one on Vista with no complaints. But if Ryan didn't think Jack could handle nineteen, he could try it himself.

All eyes riveted on leather. The referee cradled the ball, a new one that had passed the bounce test. A flick of the wrist popped it between the centers.

Edison's center resembled a toothpick—perhaps a bit thinner. He uncoiled from his crouch like a released jack-in-the-box. Dereck mistimed his leap but the ball bounded over to Moe, who tossed immediately to Ryan. The blocky forward chugged along the left side searching for an opening.

Jack raced to the far corner, then made an X-acto-knife cut for the basket. His defender tried to slide after him but his legs crossed; he slipped to his knees. Ryan gazed right at the fallen Edison player but continued to dribble. Soon the defense was back. Jack circled to his normal position for the set offense.

Before Jack could wonder about the missed opportunity, Moe bounced it in low. In the same motion that Jack grabbed it, he feinted quickly to the right. When the defender crossed his feet again, Jack accelerated to the left. Robeson had to shoot his arm out to prevent Jack from going around him.

Whistles sounded instantly.

"Foul on thirteen red." One of the referees walked to the scorer's table. "Twenty- five to the line." The visitors took inside positions for the free throw. Dereck and Ryan divided red shirts on each side of the key. Eric was going back on defense when Jack stopped him with a whisper:

"Watch me,"he said. "My man's crossing his legs on defense. I can beat him." Eric didn't answer.

"Shooting one,"the referee said. "Play the first."

Jack set his big toe carefully behind the paint. He tapped three short bounces on the gym floor, his body flexing up and down with the ball. The gym was silent, unlike the madhouse at Vista. He tried not to notice a small boy looking at him through a camera. Jack thought of Sijohn's advice.

"Just like practice,"he said to himself.

Unlike practice, though, hundreds of eyes focused on his back. He bent his knees, brought the ball in front of his face, and released it in a low arc. The ball hit the back of the rim and slid straight down with familiar "whoosh." A flash from the camera immortalized Jack's follow-through. The crowd woke up.

"Way to go."

"Keep it up!"

"Put the pressure on, Jack."

He recognized the last voice – it belonged to Jamal. At least one person honestly rooted for him today. To Jamal, Jack was a person, a friend. It was the same with Mr. Martinez, but his favorite teacher wasn't there.

To the others in the crowd, friends of Jared mainly, Jack was a bench warmer trying to fill shoes too big for him. To the majority, he was unknown. A faceless player to be judged by skill alone – how he did today, how he did right now.

Edison rushed the ball up as the home team flowed down on defense. A guard whipped a pass inside. Without a dribble, Robeson wheeled left to hook in a ten-footer. Jack loped across the end line to take the ball out. Eric stood close, his hands spread to receive the pass. Nine out of ten times, it would have gone to him automatically.

But Jack cocked his back like a quarterback. A blue jersey cut like a halfback down the middle of the court. Dereck was ahead of the pack! Jack threw it perfectly: hard enough to sting a hand but soft enough to catch.

The center, running full tilt, didn't even have to leap to make the reception. With two giant dribbles he dropped it down for two points. On the way back on defense, he pointed a finger at Jack in public gratitude. The student section again erupted. Annie, Grace and Tara tried to harness the enthusiasm into one voice.

"Here we go, Kennedy, here we go..."

"Here we go, Kennedy, here we go..."

The applause was for Dereck, but Jack made it happen. He had one foul shot, an assist, and the game had just started. Jack turned his head when a familiar voice boomed from the bench.

"Way-to-go, Jack!"Jamal hollered.

By the end of the quarter, Kennedy led by six. Robeson had all the visitor's points except two foul shots. Jack notched a basket of his own on a tip inside, rebounding seemed to be the best way to touch the ball.

Eric seemed to always work the ball into Ryan's corner. Twice Dereck heaved a pass to Jack on the weak side, but that was dangerous. When an Eagle tipped the third cross-courter, Dereck didn't try for a fourth. Jack was getting lonesome for the ball.

"Don't be satisfied,"Sijohn told them between quarters. "Keep hustling. And find some way to slow down Robeson. He's the whole team."

In the second quarter, Robeson showed why he was the league's MVP as an underclassman. Every time down, Edison tried to set up a triangle: Robeson and the thin center and a guard. Quick passes bounced around the triumvirate until someone had a shot.

If Dereck left the middle to double Robeson, the ball floated into the skinny center. Ryan fouled twice trying to pick up Dereck's man on late switches. Both times it was a three point play for Edison. The strategy put the visitors back in the lead—thirty-four to thirty.

Sijohn made one change for the second half. Jack was assigned to Robeson. Ryan had been stung by the hook too often and couldn't risk fouling out. The new starter was pulled aside into the dressing room. The coach squeezed a cold hand on the back of Jack's neck. The grip was cold, tight, reassuring. Sijohn said:

"He's bigger than you and he's stronger than you. Use your speed...and your head."

Sijohn's last word didn't make sense, and it must have showed.

"Basketball sense,"the coach explained. "Like when you fired that long pass to Dereck. You didn't plan that. Follow your instincts...they'll tell you what to do."

Jack still felt confused when he rejoined the others

for the second half. Robeson didn't look surprised when Jack stepped next to him. He was used to different opponents trying to guard him.

Edison's center extended his hand to Dereck. They grasped in a brief touch of sportsmanship. Without seeming to turn his head, Jack peered over at Robeson. The big forward made no move to shake hands.

CHAPTER 18

THE REF STOOPED between the two centers again. He tossed the ball up like a show-off chef turns a flapjack. This time Dereck sprung with perfect timing if not perfect aim. Jack bolted after the ball neck and neck with Robeson. Advantage to Jack, who was faster, over Robeson, who was stronger.

The league's leading scorer evened the odds. As they neared the ball, he pushed down with a heavy forearm. Jack stumbled to a trot, expecting a whistle. There wasn't one. Jack was twenty feet behind when the easy two points banked through the net.

The first play set the tone. Without a whistle to stop him, Robeson butted his skinny defender into the key. Sometimes body weight was enough to establish position. Sometimes Robeson pushed with his arms. Jack was posted so low to the basket he could see the net if he looked up. An easy swing with the hook put two in the bank. The pattern repeated once too often and Sijohn called a timeout. He buttonholed the officials against the scoring table.

"He's leaning on my man!"

Sijohn slashed out with his elbow, as if that's what he wanted done to Robeson. The zebras didn't buy it. They turned their backs to examine something imaginary in the scorebook. Robeson led the league in scoring, after all. This was a coach in search of a scapegoat. He could look elsewhere. Edison pounded away when play resumed. Robeson powered through defenders like a bowling ball. It was not close at the end. Even the rooters lost interest. The only unified voices of encouragement were those of Annie, Tara and Grace.

The dressing room was closed to visitors. Sijohn's three piece suit sagged open around his waist—some vest buttons had been nervously undone. The coach found the eyes of the first stringers and said simply:

"Why?"

Nobody said anything.

Neither did Sijohn.

Finally Eric was brave enough to answer. The point guard piped from the center of the room, "They had Robeson, Coach. We didn't have a stopper."

"We don't have one man,"Sijohn said. "We have five." The coach slowed down his words, as if suddenly aware the boys were younger than he thought. He stopped conversing and started lecturing.

"Basketball's a team sport. It's meant to be played as a team. Edison had one man...one man..." He paused for a moment, and Jack shifted uncomfortably—that was his man, after all. Eric didn't jump into the breach of silence this time. The coach's voice accelerated:

"There's no star on this team. Stand alone and you lose. Stand together, and there's no Robeson big enough."

Sijohn stared down Eric, trying to stifle anger. Running a hand down the front of his vest, he discovered the undone button. He unconsciously wiggled a finger through the empty notch. It seemed to act as a pacifier. His voice became less perturbed. Faint sarcasm replaced overt anger.

"If you want to play one-on-one, by all means do it. After school, before school...I don't care. But when you're representing this school, and playing for me, it's got to be together...as a team."

His head swung around the room. Even Eric didn't look back. Making his vest ship-shape with the flick of a button, he turned on his heel and vanished into the office. Dan, cradling a near empty quart of rubbing alcohol, followed the coach behind the door.

The players sat stunned. It was the first time Sijohn had been that incensed. He expected Kennedy to win, even if the players didn't. Always before, the games had rescued them from tough practices.

"Easy for him to say," said Ryan finally. "He wasn't out there."

"If we had Jared, it'd be different," added Eric. Ryan nodded. Jared would've had Robeson for lunch. "The rest of the team seemed to vouch silent agreement. Dan popped out to cancel the postmortem.

"Go home," the freckled boy said. "Orders from the boss."

The team made for the door....no arguments after a loss. Jack was almost outside when Dan grabbed his arm. He jerked a thumb toward the office. A fresh quart of rubbing alcohol was thrust on top of Jack's fist.

"Do me a favor and drop this to the coach."

Jack's fist didn't open.

"My mom's waiting,"Dan pleaded. "He talks to me after games."

Reluctantly, Jack opened his hand and closed it on the bottle. He turned and walked against the stream of players. Sijohn was sunk in his enormous leather chair. All the vest buttons were free. The waistcoat swung open like the doors of a saloon.

Jack rapped on the foggy glass of the office. He held up the new bottle of rubbing alcohol, but the coach didn't seem to see it. Sijohn's voice was subdued, barely audible.

"Sit."

Jack found the hardback chair. The cold kiss of the wood went right through to his coat. Sijohn's fingers went to the white shirt beneath his undone tie. Soon it, too, swung open.

The T shirt underneath made Jack vaguely uncomfortable, like he was stepping by a "no trespassing"sign. The coach blew out his cheeks, then asked softly:

"You know what I am?"

Jack didn't.

"A Navaho from Arizona."He blew out his cheeks again.

"Ever been on a reservation?"

Jack hadn't.

"My father was a medicine man. I'm the oldest son- an apprentice in the healing arts. Then the white man came with medical degrees. My father didn't feel like a doctor anymore."

Jack nodded and put the bottle of rubbing alcohol down. He started to back out but Sijohn spoke again.

"I decided I had to be better than the white man."He started to take off his vest. He smiled and added, "That's why my suits come in three pieces."

The disrobing continued, and Jack must have looked uncomfortable. The coach grunted dismissal. His newest starter was more than happy to get out of there.

Jack was early the next day, but Martinez had a sub. It was a woman from Canada; her Spanish tailed off into a Canadian accent. He tuned her out.

The school newspaper had come out, but none were left when zero period ended. Jack hung around in the misty air until first period. Trooping to his locker, he noticed people watching him.

He wondered why. Maybe they saw the game, Jack thought. Maybe they know how lame we are. For what- ever reason, the glances erased his usual anonymity.

He forgot his customary sneaky entrance into Chambers. The teacher snapped her newspaper down. Jack was caught, red faced, slipping into the back row. He was overdue, way overdue, for an office referral.

"I've been waiting for you,"Chambers said sweetly.

Jack waited for the other shoe to drop. Instead, she reversed her newspaper for the class to see. A skinny figure was poised under the headline, immortalized in tank top and trunks, The player's wrist was cocked down in the finish of a free throw. It was Jack, gracing the sports section, first page. The teacher dropped the paper on his desk and announced for all to hear:

"Our celebrity has arrived..."

The buzz from the class made him want to hide and made him want to preen, both at the same time. The teacher let the tardy slide. The lapse was intentional, a perk of new-found fame.

Jack made sure he was at Chambers' in plenty of time the next day. For a switch, it was Annie who scurried in with seconds to spare. The ringing bell stopped her usual visit with Tara. Near the middle of the period, she went to the correction chart. Tara wasn't far behind her. They were supposed to check their answers and sit down. Instead they talked.

At her raised desk, Ms. Chambers shifted uncomfortably. She didn't like to lower the boom on good girls, the cheerleaders. Still, this couldn't go on too long. She had to keep control, and this was a bad example. Annie didn't smile when she discovered they had company. Her mouth went straight across, no expression. She looked him in the chin again.

Jack said like a ventriloquist, "Sit down."

Annie peeked at Chambers right away. Something was up. She flashed a glance at Tara to alert her. The cheerleaders treaded away to the sanctuary of their desks. Within seconds they were diligently working on math, good girls again.

Jack lingered to write an answer, pretending to have a purpose. He swiveled around to take a step back to safety. Before he could get to his desk, the teacher's voice dropped like a fisherman's net.

"Mr. Marston..."

Jack pretended concentration on the correction chart.

"Please come to my desk."

The voice was barbed, the "please"not withstanding. He was caught—a fish yanked from warm water to cold breathless deck. Jack would do as an example—he was always coming in late anyway. The rest of the class continued work, unaware of the drama. The teacher rasped:

"Let me see your paper."

He wriggled to the control tower desk. She sized up the unfinished problem, then rolled eyes in cold disbelief.

"Do you always get the answer before you do it?"

He retracted his face down into his neck, observing under hood of eye sockets.

"No Ma'am."

He seemed sorry, but still straightforward. He froze in that penitent pose, enduring the teacher's glare for an interminable minute.

"Get to your seat,"she hissed.

The volume finally alerted the class to a happening. Pencils halted in mid-equation. In the past, it would have embarrassed Jack a lot. Ms. Chambers stared hard at the cheerleaders, too.

Annie felt it and glanced up. The teacher continued to stare. Annie's face had no expression, mouth straight across. Her nose disappeared behind the textbook.

The book tipped down as Jack passed by. A twist found its way to one corner of her mouth, then the other.

Annie looked at him curiously, straight into his eyes.

CHAPTER 19

JACK WOKE UP early on Saturday—too early. He found the clock, realized the hour, burrowed under blankets, and searched for his dream again. He was halfway to it when a rumble penetrated his pillow. Fortunately, the machinery stopped abruptly.

A slight shiver shook his legs...sleep was near. Cheerleaders drifted behind his eyes. They stood at center court, arms branched like hands of a clock at quarter to three. They sang in slow cadence like a C.D. played at wrong speed.

"Jump...Jack...Jump..."

"Jump...Jack...Jump..."

In the weirdly real world of dreams, Jack felt himself crouch for a jump ball. The crowd in the gym stayed silent, but cheerleader voices sang over and over again, slower and slower:

"Jump...Jack...Jump..."

"Jump...Jack...Jump"

The referee dipped the ball down. Jack's sleeping body twitched as he exploded after it. His feet lifted from the hardwood as if he had rockets for shoes. He reached the ball first, but didn't slap it to a teammate. Instead, he snatched it out of the air.

Jack scissored his legs like an underwater swimmer, hugging the ball against his stomach. The other players shrank and shrank as he kept going up. Unfortunately, gymnasiums by definition have a roof.

A huge beam buttressing the ceiling jutted into the flight path. Jack bounced around it and headed toward the skylight. He felt powerless, like a balloon some little kid let slip in a carnival tent. The skylight chunked him in the back. He shivered.

The game below stopped. The players pointed to the ceiling like a crowd under a suicide jumper. The safety glass mashed against Jack's uniform, a cold reminder that heaven wasn't reachable. Jared's voice emerged from the multitude :

"Let it go, Jack. We can't play if you've got the ball."

Jack squeezed the basketball in the crook of his elbow. Jared turned to the cheerleaders and slapped his hands. They obediently crouched into a slow-motion number.

"Give it back."

"Give it back."

"Give it back."

The crowd picked it up. The lips of the first stringers moved with the words. Jack hugged the ball tighter against his stomach. Once more his back shivered against the skylight. If they wanted it so badly, they could come and get it. The gym reverberated.

"Give it back."

"Give it back."

"Give it back."

The chant echoed up to the rafters, relentless as a locomotive counting train tracks in the stillest part of the night. Everyone mouthed the same words. The young voices sounded old, and it made Jack feel lonely.

"Give it back."

"Give it back."

"Give it back."

He wondered why everyone wanted the ball so much, and why he didn't want to give it up. He scanned the mob for Annie. Jack found the tail of her hair sweeping back and forth in slow time with the cheer. The ball lost its buoyancy the minute he sighted her.

It slipped from his hands. The eyes of the crowd followed it, the howl dampening to a murmur. Hitting the floor with a boom, it bounced halfway up again. Jack reached down for it, but knew it wouldn't come back once he'd lost hold.

Then he began to sink, too, slowly drifting down to be like everyone else. There was no hissing sound, like when helium escapes from a balloon. No one below noticed. The game resumed with Jared in Jack's spot. The crowd and cheerleaders went back to watching it.

Just like movies, dreams have a beginning, middle, and end. Jack knew the ride was over when he was close enough to see the cracks in the floor. Keeping his eyes shut wouldn't bring back weightlessness. His flying days were over.

Unsticking his eyelids, he marched like a robot toward the bathroom. There was a ruffle of newspapers, but Jack kicked the door open automatically. It slammed back in his face.

"Don't you ever knock?"

Jack stumbled back. The bed board hit his calves. He sat down involuntarily on the bed, up against a large duffel bag. He'd been sleeping deeply, but now he recognized the sound he'd heard. The machinery was a motorcycle. The breathing of the cylinders lingered under his consciousness like a bedsore you learn to sleep with. The door opened. Grant breezed out with newspaper in hand.

"Someone took one of these to school." <u>The Outlook</u> was tossed down to the floor. "Easy to get ink in basketball ... had to win the league before I got in."

Jack grunted. His brother was talking wrestling, of course.

"Doin' more than shootin' freethrows?"

Jack said with shy pride, "I'm starting."

Grant said, "When's the last time you were first in anything"

It wasn't a question and Jack didn't answer. Finally his brother did it for him:

"Like never."

Grant slung the duffel bag into the bathroom, then

followed it. Jack heard soft plops of laundry being dispensed into the hamper. The gentle sound speeded Jack's heart like a strong cup of coffee.

Any hope for brotherly love was gone when Grant came out.

CHAPTER 20

THE DUFFEL BAG was deflated when his brother returned. The empty sack landed on Jack's lap. Grant smiled—no mirth behind the grin.

"Still on Strike?"

Jack flipped the duffel bag to the floor and flattened it with his feet. "You just add to our work around here."

"You mean your work. This is between you and me."

"... and Mom. She still thinks you're a king."

"So?"

"We do the laundry, cook the meals, maintain the house..."

"You don't do all that,"Grant interjected. "Mom does. Since when do you..."

"Since you left."

Grant's glare flickered. "I mow the lawn."

"If we waited for that, they'd have safaris in the backyard."

Grant clenched his fingers into a ball. "When I'm home I do it."

"You make sure you're not home enough to get your hands dirty."

A finger popped out of the fist. It stuck Jack's breastbone. It hurt. Jack almost jabbed back, but took a breath instead. Hot blood was sucked back inside with the new oxygen.

It would be suicide to fight Grant. Why should he get pounded? Anger congealed inside him, like molten lava cooling in a long-dormant volcano. The forefinger pricked him again.

Jack rose to his feet unsurely. He pancaked the flat duffel bag with his feet. Grant recognized the submissive posture. The finger dropped away. Six quick steps and Jack was out the bedroom door. Grant laughed the mirthless laugh and called after him:

"Go ahead—run away. You always do."

Jack made Chamber's class right after the tardy bell on Monday—early for him. As usual, the teacher's head was safely in her purse. In thanksgiving, he buried himself in the obscurity of a math problem. It was a cinch.

Annie passed his desk on the way to the correction chart. This time he had something to correct, too. She didn't see him come up after her. He said:

"How'd you do?"

Annie looked startled. They both checked Chambers, who was still busy inside her purse. Jack said:

"I'm on the same one." He pretended to admire the problem on her paper.

She in turn looked at his paper. He wasn't on the same problem at all, not even the same page.

Jack was gazing down at her clothes—knee socks and short dress. It was almost like her cheerleading costume, but tighter in the right places.

Annie's eyes bounced again to chambers. Coast still clear. In a bare whisper she said:

"I missed it."

Any answer would have done, in any level of whisper. She was acknowledging him, answering him, talking to him. Maybe he was finally forgiven for turning down Annie's party. Jack's stomach fluttered, like before league games. He said:

"I did too."

With a shake of his head that meant goodbye, he left the chart. They couldn't leave together, like they were a pair. He dragged slow air through his lungs like a smoker trying to soothe himself with nicotine. It didn't work. He'd never get used to talking to girls.

Annie stayed at the chart another minute. A twist was at the corner of her mouth again. Jack watched the dark honey-brown hair swish back and forth on the way to her desk.

His nerves weren't settled any by a call slip that came during sixth period. The girl with braids sashayed in and dropped a blue half sheet on Jack's desk. A boy in the back groaned in a funny voice of fake fear. It didn't fool anybody—blue meant attendance office, not vice principal.

Jack surrendered the slip to a secretary in the

office. A boy who had spoken to him in the yard came up from a chair. He carried a spiral bound notebook like a badge. He said:

"I'm from the paper."

"The newspaper?"

Jack couldn't believe it. His picture was one thing—he was in the right place at the right time. A story was something else. He didn't have anything to say.

"Not the <u>Times</u>." The boy grinned. "The <u>Outlook</u>."

They went out together into the open air. It's double nice outside when everybody else is inside. They sat at an empty picnic table. The boy was Darrin Lee, the same name written under Jack's free throw picture. The face clicked into place, incognito without a camera for a nose.

"Why interview me?"

"Because you're new. You're not a bench warmer anymore."

Jared would dispute that statement. Jack looked back at the school still in session and said noncommittally, "It's nice out here."

Darrin said, "Power of the media..."

Jack thought how people noticed him in the morning, people he didn't even know.

"...nothing can stop it,"Darrin said. "It can even get you out of class." There was a silence. The reporter searched for common ground.

"You're friends with Annie..."

Jack wasn't sure.

"She's in journalism."

Jack nodded.

"Just doesn't do sports."

Jack didn't add anything to Annie's description.

Darrin said dejectedly, "Out of my league...but I can dream."

Jack nodded like she was out of both of their leagues.

"Hear she liked you."

Jack said,"That's history." Even Darrin had used the past tense.

"History repeats."

Jack shook his head. He wasn't used to being interviewed. His answers to Darrin's questions were coming out short—audible but not quotable.

Darrin said, "I'm trying to get an angle on you." This wasn't working. He couldn't seem to loosen Jack up. A bell rang. Darrin said quickly:

"You're the new kid on the block..." Students started pouring out of buildings. As the noise level rose, Darrin said, "But I need something to make a story."

Practice that day was tougher than usual. Once the whole team had to sprint around the track. Stragglers had to suffer the lash of the coach's tongue.

"We do everything together,"Sijohn yelled at their tails. Then, as if an order could make it so, he declared:

"There's unity on this team!"

The price of unity was a workout more exhausting than any game. Their eyes glossed over with fatigue during the last drill. Ryan, like a tired tug boat, plowed down the court at one quarter speed. He was either a good actor or out on his feet. Sijohn granted the benefit of the doubt. A whistle ended the torture. The first team collapsed on the benches instead of going straight for the showers. They were too tired to move.

"The Eagles will be a cinch after this,"Dereck said between gulps of air. "I can't take any more of these workouts."

Nobody said anything about it, but Jared was due back soon.

CHAPTER 21

THE HORRIFIC TONES of a female voice woke him up. When her tonsils were into it, his mother's voice could peel the paint right off the walls. The perfume of cinnamon oatmeal wafted down the hallway. That got him going—if the stick didn't work, the carrot would.

His mother was shrouded in newspaper when he joined her. Twin lunches were on the kitchen counter. She saw him looking at it and said, "Double shift tonight."

Jack frowned. So many hours are a killer.

His mother shrugged like it couldn't be helped. She gave a start as he transferred oatmeal from pot to bowl. "Listen to this,"she said.

Jack sat down and waited while a page folded back. Impatient, he dipped in for a first spoonful. His mother finally found what she was looking for and read it verbatim.

"Aries: Not giving your best will only short change

you. Feelings of self-confidence will build when you meet a current challenge. Make a request for a transfer if you're unhappy. A lover on the horizon."

"Thought you didn't believe in that stuff,"Jack said. His mother poked out from the tent of newspaper.

"Gotta believe in something, kiddo." She disappeared again into tent city.

"A lover on your horizon?"

That got a snort. She deadpanned back at him:

"You're an Aries too, young man."

Jack smirked. He had just missed being his mother's birthday present. Mrs. Marston smiled at her son's smile. He felt unaccountably happy as he spooned in a last chunk of oatmeal.

"Speaking of good, I hear you're a good basketball player."

"Who told you that?"

"It's in the stars,"she said in mock mystery.

"You mean it's in the newspaper." She already had him smiling. He couldn't get on her case for snooping around. She must have found the <u>Outlook</u> with his picture.

"Grant told me. Why didn't you tell me?"

Jack toyed with his oatmeal spoon, finally sticking it back into his mouth upside down.

His mother shrugged, then collapsed the tent of newspaper. She left in a blur of blue. The fading pat of his mother's shoes left him alone with an empty bowl. He clean-licked the spoon.

He forced himself to coast along the farm trail on the way to school. It was one thing to have a sticky shirt at home, quite another to be sweaty at school. Besides, he'd need all his energy later at practice.

Mr. Martinez, his face attached to an English essay, was already in his room. Warm air tingled Jack's ears when he opened the door. The teacher, with just a twinge of guilt, peeped over the top of granny glasses.

"Sorry I wasn't here yesterday."

Jack brushed off the excuse — it wasn't necessary.

"Flu bug got me."

Jack brushed his books down and said, "Hear about Edison?"

The game offered welcome absolution. Martinez spoke with the split concentration of someone doing two things at once. The pen drew red marks over the white paper as he talked.

"We won, didn't we?"

"No, we lost."

"And you..."

"Everybody's actin' different."

"Maybe you are different."Mr. Martinez made a final red line. "Ever think of that?"

Jack did think of it on the way to first period. People stopped talking as he passed. One short boy in a brown shirt even spoke.

"Good luck against the Eagles,"the stranger said.

Jack nodded, not knowing the boy's name.

By first period, everyone knew Jared was back.

He strolled nonchalantly through the hallways as if he hadn't missed a day. Sijohn wouldn't allow him on the team yet, but Jared couldn't afford to miss any more school and still graduate. Word was sent out for first stringers to meet before practice. Jared was already at the picnic table when Jack arrived.

"Come here,"the captain ordered. His hands played with the razor blade around his neck.

Ryan and Moe separated and Jack took the split between them. The first string shrank into a tight unit. Jared said:

"You know whose fault my suspension was?"

No one said anything. Jared answered it himself.

"Odd Dodd"

Her name was slurred, like he was mentioning a mass murderer. The chain around Jared's neck seemed to irritate him. His head ducked and the chain dislodged. The razor blade was plunged into the wood bench. It quivered for a second like a fresh arrow in a bulls eye.

"That's sharp,"said Ryan.

Jared laughed bitterly. His voice notched tighter, more conspiratorial. "You know where I'd like to put it."

"What're you gonna do?"Eric breathed. The boys contracted their leader.

She's not getting away with it,"Jared stated. "My season's spoiled...but it's not over yet." He spit out another short and sour laugh. "And I'll spoil her year."

"So what are you..."

"We" Jared corrected. "What are <u>we</u> gonna do. We're in this together. Just follow me. You'll have a good time. And nobody'll get hurt."

"Except Mrs. Dodd," Jack said to himself on the way to practice.

Annie, Tara, and Grace were in a huddle of girls when Jack came out after his shower. They had stayed late practicing cheers. Jared was still in the yard and had Grace by the hand. Jamal snagged Tara and pulled her to him. Jack hugged the walls of the school, a part of him shy and not wanting to be noticed. Strands of sunlight, fading now, blended the hue of the buildings into sameness.

When he passed between the gym and cafeteria, a last ray from the setting sun caught him in the eye. Wincing, he stepped backward out of the light. Too late—it was enough to betray his presence. The female cluster revolved like a living, thinking organism toward him.

Annie was encased within the klatch of girls, but she could be seen. She was looking at him. The roulette wheel rotated until it stopped at his own personal jackpot. When he didn't say anything, the wheel started to move again. Jack said loud so his voice would penetrate through the girls:

"Hi."

Instead of just saying it, he croaked the word deep and inhuman like a frog. There was no response except the girls stopped talking. His feet stuck in the asphalt, balanced to go backward or forward. Finally he decided on forward, if that's what you call a half-hearted step. A small stride, but definite.

The powers that be accepted it as progress. "With that cue the girls began dispersing from around Annie. The choreography advanced automatically, as if an opening movement of a complex dance.

Tara led the retreat, yanking Jamal by the hand until they were up against the science building. Grace corralled Jared who trailed like a sidewalk superintendent at a construction site.

Only Annie stood still, waiting.

CHAPTER 22

THE BLUE HAD washed out of Annie's navy sweater. The sun rays had almost receded from the yard. They seemed to be alone. Their eyes met, a steady and straight connection.

"We can't always meet at the chart,"Annie said. "Chambers will kill us."

Jack nodded—no use giving the amphibious croak a chance to return.

Her brown eyes danced over his face. It seemed like just the two of them in the yard, no security blanket to clutch. Jamal, in fact, was gone—Tara stood alone against the wall. The littlest cheerleader was hardly visible, shrinking like a child against the science lab. He focused into the distance, grabbing for something, anything, to say.

A horn honked from the street.

"Better late than never," Annie said. Her voice was suddenly taut, like a rubberband stretched to snap. She shook her hair, as if distress could be shed like unwanted dandruff. Her head tilted back to Jack. She plugged back into his eyes. The rubberband voice relaxed to a whisper.

"Bye." She walked toward the horn.

"Good bye." His words sounded formal, like he was talking to an aunt he saw twice a year.

Her hair caught an orphan gleam of sunshine. The light flickered the honey strands into a jagged halo. Her head stayed luminous over the washed out sweater, floating away in the darkness like a Chesire Cat. Then, when even that faded to outline, a voice purred from nowhere.

"See you in math."

Annie entered the night. Her shadow united with Tara's silhouette. Both disappeared to black. A car door slammed. An engine gunned. She was gone.

Jack pivoted toward the bike racks. He thought something moved near the picnic tables. By squinting, he could just make out Jared and Grace. They weren't standing close enough to have been kissing, yet they weren't talking either. Jared didn't need a security blanket for lapsed conversations. They had been listening, and Jack didn't know why.

The cruise home was uneventful enough. He pumped the pedals of his bike like a madman—his legs weren't heavy from the scrimmage anymore. When the big ditch came up, Jack had a notion to sail right over it, like E.T. shooting across a Halloween moon. That was crazy—even the narrow throat of Bottoms Up went a long way down. The future loomed too exciting to have it disappear down a hole.

He carefully edged around the pit. It was so dark the handlebars at the bottom were invisible. Gazing into the canyon, he thought of his brother. Jack had a feeling he'd had his last motorcycle flight.

With the ditch was behind him, he pumped hard against the incline until he reached home. Perspiration covered his body, sticking his shirt to him with smelly glue. He felt as if he'd scored the winning basket in a championship game.

He dreamt that night of Annie and the Eagles.

It seemed like forever before the next game. Practices became habit, like rote math drills. At the end of Tuesday's practice Sijohn blew his whistle for free throw drills. The players attached the ball bag like it was full of treasure. Jack didn't care to muscle into the pack around Dan. The team scavenged the sack for the best balls, then scattered to baskets.

There was one ball left when Jack got there. The seam was split slightly—the rubber bladder bulged through with a black smile. A grin creased through Dan's freckled cheeks.

"First come, first served."

As if to prove the worthiness of his product, Dan dropped it into a test bounce that always made Dan's day. His cheeks inflated further, carving twin canyons through the freckles.

"Like I said..."

Jack interrupted. "You rebound, funnyman."

Sijohn moved into the stands. Darrin was already

sitting in the top row, feet stretched to the bench ahead. The reporter's camera bag formed a hard pillow against the wall behind him. The coach sidearmed a wave to the media, then reclined in a middle row.

Everyone knew the drill. Shoot 25, keep going until you miss, then hit the showers. Jack fingered the ball dubiously, like it was leftover melon on sale in a supermarket.

All the tread had been worn away. It felt slick without the inverted dimples that give traction to fingertips. He punched the not-quite-round ball down with some harshness. It must have hit a sweet spot, for it came up straight.

Only a side basket was left, the worst one. The backboard was dead. The paint was chipped. The hoop was loose. Dan stationed himself directly under the torn net—no question as to where the ball was coming down. He spread his arms like a father waiting for a little girl to come down a slide.

Jack took a step forward and went straight up for a fifteen foot jumper. It came out the hole in the net. Dan fisted it back out.

Over Dan's shoulder, Sijohn's face wrinkled. Jack could read the thought. Do it like a game—don't shoot jumpers from the line.

Jack spun the next one around his palms and shot it right. Same result. Dan jabbed it out like a fighter at a speed bag. Today the rhythm was there.

...find the seam...

...hunch the back...

...straighten the arm...

...snap the wrist...

25 went down. Behind Jack, the balls slowed their bounces. Arms wet the perspiration, it was hard to hit too many in a row. Everyone finished but Jack.

Sijohn glanced at his watch. Darrin took the camera bag pillow from behind his back. Jack blocked them out. He searched for a seam, crouched, released. Then he did it over again, exactly the same.

...30...31...32...

Balls stopped bouncing. Shoes stopped squeaking. Sijohn took two steps down and looked at his watch. Darrin explored his camera bag as if suddenly inspired. The reporter passed the coach with a rush, a camera looped around his neck like a slackened noose. Dan punched the ball out faster.

...44...45...46...

Eyes attached to Jack's back, then left to watch the ball kiss the net. It was becoming a performance. The attention didn't worry Jack. Pressure was trying to do something you couldn't do. He could do this. Dan kept batting it out and Jack kept putting it in.

...54...55...56...

Sijohn's shoes hit the parquet floor, pawing at it like a counting horse. Finally he called out, "I've got to turn out the lights, Jack. Ten more is it."

Silence met the ultimatum. Jack wondered if they wanted to see him miss. They'd have a long wait. Darrin set up behind the basket, a little to the side of Dan. The camera came up.

...63...64...65...

Darrin peered at Jack with the Cyclops's eye. Dan held the ball and barked over his shoulder:

"75, Coach. Let him get 75."

Sijohn nodded.

Jack felt the slickness for a seam—any would do except where the rubber bladder poked through. He crouched his back, stiffened his arm, followed through with his wrist.

...72...73...74...

The seventy-fifth left his hand with a popgun sound like electronic fizz. Jack's tongue poked out of his mouth just as a light flashed.

Darrin put the camera down from his face. It might have broken Jack's concentration, but there was nothing in life to concentrate on.

As the previous 74 had done, the ball went in.

CHAPTER 23

WHEN HE GOT home that night he discovered his mother's twin lunches still on the counter. She had left for the double shift without them. Jack sank his teeth into an apple, then tied the ends of the plastic bags together. He flipped them over his shoulder like a saddlebag. He remounted his bike. All those hours were too long to go without eating.

The hospital was six stories of white stucco. Jack chained his bike to an iron guard rail, reshouldered the saddlebags, and went through double white doors. He waved by the volunteer at the hospitality desk and followed a blue arrow painted down the center of the hall.

After twists and turns the arrow petered out at an elevator. The lift was wide and deep enough to hold a surgical trolley—no claustrophobia here. He punched the button marked number 6.

When the door opened on the sixth floor, he unshouldered the bags. He approached the nurses' station. A large woman was behind a counter, behind a desk, behind a lamp, finally behind glasses tinted pink.

Jack looked her over and waited to be noticed. Her hair was the same color as her white scrubs; both had starchy, cardboard stiffness. She might have felt his eyes. The helmet of hair moved up and back, but the face went down again. The woman's skin gave off a faint sheen—oily make-up or perspiration.

Broomhead, Jack thought, this is Broomhead.

He manufactured the kind of cough people do for recognition. No reaction. There was no subtle way to get through. She'd constructed layer upon layer of protection against trouble like him.

"Excuse me,"Jack said.

The pink eyes reluctantly raised, looked him over, dropped. He was nobody important. Maybe he'd go away.

"Excuse me,"Jack said again.

This time the head jacked up with the eyes, the chin dropped down, the throat wrinkled. She muttered at the intruder a name—his mother's name.

"Sally."

No answer came. The large white mass of womanhood migrated sideways in her throne. She was used to being obeyed. His mother was just another layer of protection between her and trouble.

"Sally,"she repeated.

A little itty-bitty voice said, "yes."

Jack didn't know that voice. Sally came out the back. She saw Jack and gave the trademarked mother's look that says, What's wrong?

Jack held up the saddle bagged lunches. The face relaxed. The itty-bitty voice lowered, like they were in church instead of a nurse's station.

"Jack, you shouldn't have..."

The contrast between work voice and home voice was startling. It was distinct enough, perfectly understandable, but so respectful that it made the speaker fragile.

Jack thought to himself, she's afraid of this woman. He slapped the food bags on the counter, perhaps a little too hard. One of the halves slid too far and teetered over the ledge. Something heavy was in there, a coke or something, for it dragged the other bag with it onto the floor.

Jack wasn't tall enough to belly over the counter and get it. It was close enough for the big woman to easily pick up and hand back. She didn't move a hair on her helmeted head. It made Jack mad, so he said over-politely:

"I don't think we've met. You must be Broomhead."

"Brumhaus," his mother said quickly, as if that one word could break her into pieces. "Mrs. Brumhaus."

He had achieved the big woman's full attention. A mottle of pink showed under ivory makeup. She stood up slowly, like an ocean liner leaving its berth for a transatlantic run. Fierce little eyes tuned on him again. They were the eyes of a raptor, someone who lives off weaker animals.

Jack looked right back at her, but not like a prey.

He could be assertive, if it was for his mother. Sally was fumbling on the floor after the tumbled bag. She didn't have it in her to fight back against the boss. "Thanks honey,"Sally mumbled, "See you later."She got up, turned and creeped back to her area, and Jack sighed and slowly walked backed to the elevator and pushed the red down button.

Annie, Jared, and Grace were in the hallway on the way to Chamber's the next morning. The trio formed a small damn around the incoming tide of students. Grace had Jared's neck in a gentle hammerlock.

Annie's back was to Jack as he went by. She cradled her cheeks with both palms; Jared waved his own around for emphasis. The captain was trying to convince her of something. The eloquence whirlpooled away in the rush hour vortex of noise. Jared saw Jack slide by, but Annie didn't.

"What if he won't go?"

"Oh come on,"coaxed Grace. "You won't know if you don't try."

The tide of students washed Jack by before he knew what they were talking about. He made Chambers' in plenty of time. It was Annie who scurried in just seconds before the bell. She smiled and tilted her face like the night before.

Near the middle of the period, Annie went to the correction chart. Jack grabbed his paper. Annie smiled a second time when she discovered she had company. His stomach rumbled a greeting for him, like far away thunder.

Annie murmured an almost silent greeting.

Jack mumbled something back to cover the groan from his belly. She didn't seem to mind. Her lashes blinked up to see if the teacher was watching. Chambers' sagged against her desk in a sleepy horse stance. Annie's brown eyes escaped into Jack's blue ones.

"I'm having another party,"she said.

Jack's head bobbed down as his heart jumped up.

She whispered, "You're invited."

Jack didn't see his mother until the next evening. She wasn't so much thankful for the lunch as perturbed that Brumhaus had been called Broomhead. Just a slip of the tongue, Jack said. Besides, he didn't care. The woman with the cardboard hair was rude.

"I think you're afraid of her,"Jack said.

"If I was afraid, would I have this?"

An official looking paper lay on the table. Jack picked it up. "Sally Marston"was neatly printed inside the top rectangular box. He heard his mother sing over the kitchen stove. Two shifts at work and she still had a song left.

Jack said, "What is it?"

The song over the stove upped in volume. His eyes returned to the paper. Block letters on top told him it was an application. A second look said it was completely filled out. A third look told him Broomhead was the target.

"Gonna turn this in?"

"Soon." She extended the double O's like a song

lyric.

"Go after old Broomhead!"

"I'd be her equal, Jack. She'd still be there."

She went back to singing and stirring. Jack waited a while, trying to decide something. It didn't take long. No more regrets. No more invitations shredded to confetti. He was going this time. He was afraid, but he was going anyway. When he spoke, his words cleaved like the tip of a sharp knife.

"I'm going to a party."

The song went dead. His mother stopped stirring. She licked the spoon. A drop came off and hit the stove. She didn't wipe it up.

"Only a matter of time," she said.

He worried she was going to tease. Now he almost hoped she would.

"I mean it's only natural..."

"No big deal, Mom..."

His mother sighed. They both knew better than that.

He mentioned Annie, the sudden invitation in math.

"RSVP this time," she said. "We can eat later." Resignation languished into her voice, the first fortification to change. The flame was lowered under the pot. She came back with her cell phone and left it on the table.

Jack picked up the phone. The refrigerator door opened. Ice cubes collided in an empty glass. The second fortification to change.

He punched in the number....remembering it from the first invitation. Best to get it over with. In the other room, chilled wine splashed over ice. The phone was answered on the third ring. It was Annie. Her voice was soft, serene. It made him stutter.

What Jack lacked in style was covered by speed. The acceptance was ventilated by short puffs of breath. He wasn't used to this—it was worse than guarding Robeson. When he ran out of words, Annie picked up the slack.

"I know it's kinda quick...this weekend and all. But everyone just convinced me."

Jack held up his end of the conversation with a cough.

"Still gotta talk to my parents. My mother's never here."Her voice went down a notch, as if this was special invitation. "You're the first to know...I mean, officially."

Jack could hear himself breathe. His lungs contracted with an unhealthy wheeze. Air whisked around the phone like a vacuum cleaner in reverse.

"Bye,"she purred finally. Jack wondered if girls practiced talking that way, in the smooth sibilance of promise.

"Goodbye,"he said, unconsciously scratching the reserve meant for an acquaintance, not a girlfriend. He hung up, but sat still.

A girlfriend? Jack Marston with a girlfriend? A cheerleader girlfriend, no less. It sounded foreign, as foreign as being first string with Jared back.

The flame under the pan had gone completely out when Jack returned. His mother sat with a tall glass of wine. Her voice came out cold, like the ice cubes in the bottom of the glass.

"Is it set?"

The voice sent shivers down his back. He nodded. She clicked the stove back on. Blue gas flames appeared to hold the pot with flickering fingers. He looked for the curtain in her eyes, but didn't find it. The sadness came from within, not the wine.

"It's only natural, you know." She picked up her glass for reassurance. She sucked a swallow, searching for something wet between shrunken hunks of ice.

"Boys grow up,"she said. She dropped her eyes to the application without seeing it. "They leave."

"I'm not Grant."

The touch to reality wavered, like an FM station that didn't quite come in.

"It starts with girls,"Mrs. Marston said.

The clean nurse's nails zigzagged an "X"on the application for Broomhead's job. It was like she was putting an evil mark on it, a bad luck sign.

The second slash flipped it away. It swirled to the edge of the table, teetered, then glided back and forth to the floor. Withdrawal was his mother's armor, a retreat to status quo. The curtain dropped finally and coldly down her eyelids.

Jack retrieved the application off the floor. He positioned it carefully on a corner of the dining room table. She stared at it blankly, not seeing it anymore.

The girl with the braids sashayed into sixth period the next day. Another blue call slip landed on Jack's desk. Darrin was in the office waiting for him. They went out to the picnic table again. The reporter got right to business.

"You don't miss many free throws..."

"Don't shoot many."

"But you don't miss..."

Jack's face said neither yes nor no.

"Don't you feel pressure, standing all alone out there?" The reporter shuffled through wrinkled papers—old box scores from a bound scorebook. He finally found the sheet he wanted.

"Coach picked you to shoot a "T"against Vista."

Jack peered over and saw a small lonely circle after his name.

"...you make it?"

They both saw an "X"in the middle of the circle.

"Took you right off the bench..."

Jack added, "...and back on it,"but he couldn't help thinking of those fluttering towels.

"How many you missed this year?"

Jack shrugged.

Darrin flapped the old score sheets as he scanned them again. The pages winged back and forth in his hand. Finally his fingers pinched the pages of the notebook so they were still. He grinned like he'd captured a white butterfly, the kind that never land.

"Book says you're perfect."

Jack shrugged again.

"Ever gonna miss?"

The bell rang. The binder closed, then opened again as Darrin put in a final notation. Jack was already off the bench, packing up.

Almost to himself the reporter mumbled, "Thanks for the angle...I might have a story yet."

CHAPTER 24

JARED HAD BEEN showing up after practice, but he was careful to avoid Sijohn. He saw Jack looking for Annie by the picnic table.

"A man without his woman," he said in jest.

Jack laughed with him. He was in on jokes now, not an outsider wondering if they were on him.

Jared turned to Grace. She waved out to the street. Annie was waiting at the curb alone. She wavered a bit when she perceived a male approaching, then brightened when she saw it was Jack. Her arms loosened from a defensive tightness.

"Somebody forgot to pick me up."Annie glanced down the street. The arms dropped to her sides. "I get scared at night."

She strayed close to him, without touching. His protectiveness flared like he was a caveman with a club. Annie said, "I'm ready to give up."She waited for Jack to say something. He didn't.

"Jack..."The hint of a question hung on the end of his name. "Would you walk me home?"

Jack shortened his stride to fit her pace. He'd leave his bike at school and pick it up on the way home. The wind whisked by with a cold blast. It gave Jack the idea of putting his arms around her.

When they rounded the corner, the moon popped into view. It was round and yellow as a traffic light stuck between stop and go. He let his idea drop in the dimness. This wasn't a party, just an empty street on a weekday evening.

When they turned the next corner the moon hid behind gray gauze of cloud cover. Her hand grazed his as they changed direction. The brush made his feelings tangible. His fingers almost by instinct closed around hers.

She blinked in surprise, but didn't look at him.

For a second, her hand felt like an egg that could break with too much compression. His fingers loosened, letting her go, unconsciously making a fist without her. Their union was an embryo that could be crushed in to tight a grip.

Annie's eyes went to the hidden moon. Her hand wedged back into Jacks fist.

His fingers weakened, letting her in.

"I'm glad you're coming to my party."She squeezed his hand slightly.

Jack examined the sidewalk. He felt the long nails entwine through his.

She said, "It was Jared's idea to have it. He's such a

nice guy — he can talk me into anything."

The blocks slipped away unnoticed as they walked. They didn't stop touching until they reached the porch. The outside light was on, but the house was dark.

"Somebody forgot me,"Annie said tiredly, as if a family custom. She rummaged through her purse but couldn't find a key. She took his hand again and sat in the step.

Jack was gently pulled down beside her, as she didn't let go of the hand. A streetlamp blinked on, staring back at them from across the street. The sudden illumination violated the comfort of silence. Jack forced himself to speak.

"My mom works all the time,"he blurted.

Annie's eyes dislodged from the streetlamp.

Jack said, "I do all the work around the house. My brother does nothing."

Annie's eyes disappeared into him, like the moon into that gray gauze cloud.

Jack stopped. He was getting too personal. Why should Annie care about his home life? He was thinking how to change the subject when she said:

"I like it when you talk to me, Jack."He felt another squeeze on his hand. "You don't have to be quiet."

He looked at her without comprehension.

"You can be honest with me... tell me things nobody else knows."She compressed his hand again. "It makes us special."

Annie shook her hair as if to brush some of the

seriousness away. Her head inclined up, eyes half shutting. A car's motor was the only sound, growing louder.

The high-beams of an automobile pierced the semidarkness. A car turned into the driveway. Twin halogen spotlights scoured the house with white shafts of light.

"That's Mom,"Annie said, eyes opening all the way. The lights finished their search of the house and disappeared into the garage.

Jack got up quickly.

"Stay...I'll introduce you."

Jack started to remove himself from the porch by stepping backwards.

"Wait..."

Annie darted her face toward his like a hummingbird pulling nectar from a hard to reach flower. The kiss went against his cheek soft as a brush from a feather. Annie stepped back on the porch- gone before he could react.

Jack lost his balance and stumbled in the other direction. He didn't fight the momentum and kept walking. She watched until he turned the corner.

On the way home, he wore the mark like a pink tattoo. His hand traced over his cheek, massaging the grease of lipstick. His family would have a field day if they saw it.

The gym was still lighted when Jack got back to his bike. Sijohn was just coming out of the door, running shoes replaced by glossy boots. He filled the doorway, ponderous with the authority of a few extra inches.

The coach flicked the gym light off and another switch on. Over the gym door, a filament in a clear lightbulb ignited into brightness and revealed Jack.

"Next week,"Sijohn said, "It's the Eagles."

Jack unwrapped his bike chain.

"One thing", the coach said.

Jack wound the chain under the saddle.

"Jared might be back."

Jack didn't look up from the bike.

"You OK with that?"

Jack nodded at his bike.

A key was turned in the door. Sijohn stepped into the yard, unblocking the door. The full force of the naked lightbulb flooded over Jack. Sijohn squinted.

"What's on your cheek?"

Jack turned his head, trying to conceal the cheek in question. A knuckle raced up and down over his face. When the knuckle was glossy pink and the cheek was not, he said:

"Nothing."

The coach peered inquisitively. He wasn't that old. He could recognize pink lipstick when he saw it. High cheekbones climbed higher in amusement.

Jack applied all his weight to a bike pedal and coasted off.

CHAPTER 25

THE NEXT DAY was the weekend. The application for Broomhead's job was still carefully positioned on the corner of the dining room table. His mother didn't feel like talking and he didn't press it. For once, Jack didn't know how to brighten her up. She remained sunk in suspended animation.

Doing the lawn might cheer her up. She loved to get him working. He dragged the mower out of the garage. It was the one chore Grant was supposed to do. The idea stuck in his craw like foul-tasting medicine that took its time going down.

He clattered the machinery against the cement. Might as well get some credit for this. There was a flutter around the kitchen window. His mother's face appeared, cowled by curtains like a nun. The attempted smile came through force of will. She was a survivor.

The grass shaved off dewey, wet and sticky. The whirring blades accumulated a green coat of rye. Finally, the wheels jammed up, full of green tar. Jack stopped to flick some of it out with his fingers. When he straightened again, Grant was by the sidewalk. Jack glanced at the window...his mother was there again. Her apathy dissolved like a bad dream in morning light.

The leather jacket was flung on the dining room chair. A satchel of dirty clothes was excreted beneath. Grant didn't offer to help with the lawn. In fact, Jack stayed out of the way completely. He didn't need a Ph.D. to know they shouldn't be alone together. Jack was bundling up to get out of the house when the phone rang.

"You'd better get it, Grant,"his mother said. Then in jovial resignation, "It's probably for you."

His brother's popularity, even on occasional visits, was well established. A network of callers--usually female—went on Grant alert whenever he set foot in town.

Grant sprang to the phone and uttered a deep-voiced greeting. The next words came out softer, indicating a feminine connection. Jack was halfway out the door when the voice went hard again.

"You want to talk to who?"

He frowned into the phone. Mrs. Marston rose from the table. Jack almost had the door shut.

"You gotta be kidding."The phone juggled to the other ear. "My little brother?"

Jack shut the door, but with himself on the inside. He entered the dining room.

In a bolt of self-enlightenment, Grant said suspiciously, "Hey, what're you selling? We got plenty of magazines."

Mrs. Marston sat down again. A smile bookended her lips. Jack glided down the hallway and snapped the phone away. Capping it with his palm, he straightened in shy pride.

"Don't you have something else to do?"

His brother squinted like a strange creature had just materialized in the hallway. Their mother broke into a toothy grin, as if this was staged for her amusement.

"Since when do girls call you?" Grant squeezed his eyes at the alien being before him.

The maternal amusement spilled over into a soft laugh. The jocularity escaped her sons. Jack's palm suctioned tight over the phone. They didn't need to advertise his ignorance of the opposite sex. Annie'd find that out soon enough.

Grant heard his mother titter. He didn't like it, but didn't know what to do about it. The two brothers gazed across a vast chasm marked by time and space.

"Excuse me," he said, loading up the first word with sarcasm. Grant looked hard and long at Jack like he was a visitor from Mars. He stomped back to the kitchen, but refused to sit next to his irrepressible mother.

Jack strolled out of the room and into the hallway. He tried to shut the door for privacy, but had to crack it a smidgen for a little cool air. The cold wall bumped against his back. He slid down it until his butt hit the floor. He said hello. Annie's answer strung together like one sentence.

"Who was that...Is this a bad time...I just called to

say when the party'd start."

On the other side of the door, Grant was stewing. His mother couldn't wipe her face clean of merriment. Not wanting to be laughed at, he said finally:

"What's so funny?"

"Things are changing fast around here." She waited until the angles of her cheeks were as close to serious as they were going to get. "I just never realized..."

"Cuz a girl called? She's probably a dog."

"Maybe..."

"Maybe nothing." Jack's species of girlfriend was not in doubt. His kid brother had to start with mongrels.

Mrs. Marston gave an appropriate pause. She articulated with slow understatement.

"Of course I haven't seen her but..."

Grant said with impatience, "It's bow-wow time." He gave a comical bark. His tongue lolled out of his mouth like a sloppy puppy.

"Grant...please!"

For Jack's sake, sequestered behind the door, her voice descended to a stage whisper. The enunciation was clear enough—she objected to the animal act.

That reaction was what Grant wanted. Panting like a thirsty dog, he embellished his imitation. Softly and deliberately, Mrs. Marston said:

"Grant...she's a Kennedy cheerleader."

It was like she had turned the fire off under a hot air balloon. Grant slowly deflated into the kitchen chair like an empty bag of gas. He remembered the doggy impersonation, still preserved on his face.

With an unintentional slurp, his tongue sucked back into his mouth. The canine vanished so fast it looked amphibious, like a frog whiffing after a missed fly. He knew he looked silly, but couldn't smile at himself. Older brothers laughed; they weren't laughed at.

The face across the table was doing just that—laughing at him. They both knew dogs weren't elected cheerleaders. She'd set him up, and her own jokes were the ones she enjoyed most.

Grant's eyes bounced away in irritation. His gaze wandered to where the hallway door was a little ajar. Annie must have said something funny, for Jack's laughter carried through the door. Grant decided on a different line of attack.

"He's not washing my clothes. The laundry's his job."

"He washes mine." She retained the understatement left from the stab at comedy. She wanted to soften the confrontation now.

"Well, he's not doing mine. I'm family."

"You're never home. And when you are home, you don't..."

Grant interrupted grimly. "We're talking about Jack."

There was another pause. The lift in his mother's cheeks finally gave way, sagging into soberness. Her mirth was exchanged for his melancholy. She summoned up the nerve to answer her oldest son.

"He does the yard. That's supposed to be your job."

The words hit like a frictionless slap in the face. She'd always let it slide before, fearing responsibility would keep him away. There was silence. Grant got up and left the kitchen.

The only distraction was the lilt of Jack's laughter, flowing indistinctly through the hall door.

CHAPTER 26

Mrs. Marston found her older son in the dining room. He was gazing blankly out the window at his motorcycle. One sleeve of his leather jacket dangled on an arm; the other dragged between his legs like a beaten dog's tail.

She hovered for an instant, thinking how to change the subject. The application for Broomhead's job balanced on the table where Jack had left it. She fingered it, hesitated, came up beside her son. He wouldn't turn his head to look at her. She rumpled the paper so that it crackled under his ear. He still wouldn't bite.

"Aren't you curious?"

Grant wouldn't turn his head, much less answer.

"It's a job application."

He bit this time, tilting his head, interested.

"At the hospital,"she said. "A promotion. Jack says I should go for it."

The hair covering his temples seemed to move. He

turned directly to his mother, but his voice came in curves.

"Well, if Jack says to do it, there isn't any doubt."

The trailing leather sleeve was speared with a right arm, the indecision over. Grant bolted away—like he did when he first went for the phone—but this time he was leaving his family. He threw words back at her like darts.

"If Jack says do it, do it. He's the man."

He scooped up his untouched laundry. The front door slammed. The sack was bludgeoned against the backrest of the motorcycle. A key was fished out of a back pocket, then jammed into a slot over the tank.

His mother opened the door to go after him, but cold wind blew her back to the door stoop. Shuddering visibly, she folded bare arms against her cotton dress. Grant turned the key when he saw her lips move. He didn't want to hear it.

The cycle escalated into a growl. Obscuring any chance of human exchange. He twisted the handle all the way. The engine boiled into a paroxysm of rage. No lawnmower could hide the sound this time.

The brother left inside could hardly hear his own voice, much less the one on the line. When the engine kept revving, Jack screamed into the phone, "I'll call you back!" He felt bitter weather invade the house as he drew closer to his mother.

When Grant saw them together, he kicked the horses into gear. He reined up on one wheel, commanding the middle of the road like a drag strip. A souvenir of his visit smoked on the driveway—a strip of hot rubber. Jack didn't speak until his brother was a distant drone on the highway.

"What's this all about?"

His mother's eyes remained out on the empty street. Then, by pieces, she caved in with sadness. Jack touched her shoulder. He pulled her into the house before she caught cold.

The warmth inside revived her physical powers. She went straight back to the table and picked up Broomhead's application. She waved it in front of her face as if it were a punched train ticket. Jack had a feeling she was going to rip it up. Instead, it was folded in half, then fourths, then eighths. The document geometrically shrank to an atomized piece of nothing.

He thought she'd keep folding it until it disappeared from their lives completely. Finally, the folds wouldn't bend anymore. A fat, square-shaped, bent-up scrap was tucked into the corner of her purse—deep inside, near the bottom.

All was not forgotten the next morning. The rawness of his brother's departure haunted them. The driveway skid mark was a ghostly touch of Grant's presence. It was more than rubber on a sidewalk. It itched in their minds like a scab that couldn't be scratched because it might bleed.

Oatmeal was steaming on the table when he got there. His mother watched him eat it. She seemed to share Jack's sustenance, as if saying, "I can still be a mother to you." He felt vague guilt and put his spoon down.

JACK'S BACK

"Where's yours?"

"No time. One of the girls got sick...double shift."

Her lunch was on the counter—actually two meals: lunch and dinner. Cafeteria food was a fate worse than death—his mother just wouldn't eat it. He refilled his spoon and said:

"That's not fair. Tell Broomhead to leave her desk and actually visit a patient."

His mother looked at him like he had said something exactly wrong. Jack's spoon was loaded and unloaded twice before she said:

"Who told you life was fair?" Her face pooched in like she was squinting against the sun. "Not me."

He unloaded the spoon for a last time, then mashed the cereal down with a stab of stainless steel. A little crater opened in the oatmeal and milk poured into it. Jack hadn't meant to hurt, only to protect. She had seen a husband depart, now a son. The abandonment had imprinted her like a stigmata that could bleed at the slightest touch.

She left the room, then shuttled back in with a purse. Her movements were stiff and automatic as a zombie come to life. His mother left for work in that depressed condition. She wouldn't be home for so many hours. Hours like that could numb the mind to life's unfairness.

It was at school that Jack first heard about it. Mr. Martinez unearthed a newspaper from beneath a pile of essays. He threw it in front of Jack like a particularly witty paragraph.

"Read this."

His eyes twinkled through square-framed glasses. He picked up his red pen and made trillionth mark on a millionth essay. It was the <u>Outlook</u>, so fresh the ink still smelled.

Jack's picture was on the front page, not the sports section. Once again he was shooting a free throw, but this time wearing a practice jersey. His tongue was pointing out between his teeth. Underneath was a caption the size and thickness used for presidential assassinations.

WILL HE EVER MISS?

Jack thought of those phony headlines anyone could buy—the kind that say JOE BLOW WINS MAN OF THE YEAR. He scanned the story. It described the day he was hot from the line, the day Dan fed it out as fast as Jack could put it in. Was this for real, or a joke? He looked at Martinez for a clue. The granny glasses tipped down. Red pen lodged into a fist.

"Advance copy,"he said. "Not officially out 'til tomorrow."

Jack snared Darrin after third period. The reporter flashed a wicked snake-eyed grin and said, "What're you talking about? Everybody likes their picture in the paper."

Jack said hotly, "You made it a joke."

He wanted to articulate the injustice. The giant headline, the placement on the first page, the mock seriousness of the story, Jack's image for all to judge. But Darrin knew all that, of course. He had thought of it.

The first bell rang and Jack only had time to mumble:

"It was just practice. It didn't mean anything."

"Power of the media," Darrin said. "It can even make you a star."

CHAPTER 26

AS SIJOHN PROMISED, Jared was back at practice.

He strolled out nonchalantly, as if he hadn't missed a day. He shot around at the starters' basket wearing the starters' blue jersey. Wisecracking with old friends, he bantered the suspension around like it was a holiday. The enforced vacation sounded like summertime fun.

The coach whistled the team over. He made a scuff on the floor with his running shoe, then announced the obvious. The Eagles would be next. The boys knew that, and didn't look up. The inattention didn't bother Sijohn. He outlined the rest of the league, saving the best teams for last. The Mountaineers and Ventura, both undefeated, would play each other next.

Warm sweat turned cold on Jack's back. Jack thought of Ventura. He remembered the final soccer game, the one he'd blown. A muscle involuntarily twitched a shoulder. He closed his eyes and tried to visualize anything but the soccer fiasco.

Sijohn ordered a warm-up lap around the track. Jared wedged into the pack, emerging in tight formation with the leaders. Eric and Ryan closed around him like he had reclaimed a natural spot. Jack faded into place behind the first string. A scrap of conversation floated back.

"Now we'll fly,"Eric said. "The Eagles don't have a chance."

When they hit the gym again, the team instinctively divided itself. Jack maneuvered next to Jamal. Would "Jamal's team"become "Jack's team"once more? The two squads surveyed each other like old sparring partners ready to have at it.

Jack took his shirt off and pulled it inside out. The gold color seemed faintly foreign. Gold against blue, and he was gold again. The fit was the same—it only looked different. Eric stood ready to take it out when the whistle screeched.

"Jack,"Sijohn ordered gruffly. "Switch back with Jared."

Jack peeled off his jersey again, reversing it to blue. When his head came out of the neck hole, he saw Jared. He was standing with his shoulders back, shirt untouched.

"Well..."Sijohn said.

Jared didn't move.

"Waiting for an engraved invitation?"

Jared still didn't move. The hands at his side crunched into fists.

Sijohn's face went frigid. The two practice squads

watched, an invisible, uncrossable line between them. First string against second string. No one had to tell Jack the side he was on, the side he'd always been on. No one had his back. It was a state of mind that couldn't be assigned by a coach. Sijohn's voice declined to minus-Fahrenheit.

"I'm going to tell you one more time. After that you might as well..."

"It's OK,"Jack interrupted. "I don't mind."

"You don't mind what?"the coach snapped.

"Being second string."

"You'll play where I tell you to play."

"I was just thinking of the team..."

"Let him finish,"Jared said. He looked at Jack with acceptance. "He's got he right idea."

"Come to my office,"Sijohn blared, his temper erupting. He strode off with head high, oblivious to the boys across his path. The team divided like the Red Sea before Moses. The coach swiveled at the office door.

"Jack, you come in when Jared comes out."

The office door clanked shut before Jack got there. Jared and Sijohn were alone inside. Jack leaned against the stucco partition. A low murmur permeated the wall like it was made of terrycloth instead of stucco.

"Go back to the floor and do what I say. Or go home and stay home."

Jack listened for a response and heard none. He wished his turn would come. Getting yelled at was no picnic, but the worst part was waiting to get yelled at.

The coach's voice blasted again:

"You've got one choice to make."

There was an indistinct mumble.

"I can't hear you,"Sijohn said.

"I want to play!"This time Jared screamed back louder than the coach.

The volume was apparently satisfactory. The door snapped open. Jared froze for an instant under the archway, as if surprised his rival would be there. His eyebrows arched, eyes flamed. He brushed by and attacked the stairs three at a time. He just disappeared when Sijohn hollered again.

Now it was Jack's turn.

CHAPTER 27

THE ROOM SMELLED of Dan's rubbing alcohol, more like a training room than a coach's office. The hard backed chair was in front of the desk, but Jack had no thought of sitting. His back stiffened in anticipation of what happened to Jared. Sijohn was sunk in the oversize leather chair. His voice came out in a throaty whisper.

"Why don't you get out of your own way?"

Jack shuffled his feet and waited for more. The coach diminished into the cushions. The ramrod-straight marionette that strutted through practice had vanished. The coach flicked a finger toward the hard-backed chair. Jack sat, the backrest making him bend forward, hands on knees.

"You know why I put up with Jared?"

Jack didn't.

"He fights. Sometimes I don't like the way he fights...but he fights."

Sijohn sucked a lip between his teeth, then sat up with a trace of old stiffness. His voice rasped like a godfather with a life or death decree.

"You don't fight at all."

One of Jack's elbows slipped off a knee. He collapsed forward, as if shrinking from the pronouncement.

"I'm not talking fist fights, but...hell...you don't even resist. You go along with it."He scrutinized Jack's slouched posture. "What do you think Jamal'd give to start?"

Jack knew the answer. He'd die for it.

"You just want to belong...is that it?"

The lids over Jack's eyes locked down, almost of their own accord, shutting out the world. When they opened again, he saw only floor. A cold blank of concrete stared back at him, like a summary of the past.

Some papers were ruffled on the desk in a vague dismissal. Jack's elbow found a knee again and he straightened. He wasn't sure it was over, so he didn't get up. Sure enough, the coach remembered something else.

"The last time you were here,"he said hoarsely, "I started babbling about my roots. You got nervous, so I let you go." The thought passed through Jack's head that the rubbing alcohol hadn't really been needed. Dan's subtle mission was to get Jack in to see the coach.

"I wanted to talk about pressure."

Jack shifted cheeks on the hard chair. It was better than what happened to Jared.

"Plenty of pressure where I grew up, but no jobs. People gave up."

Jack shifted again uneasily in the chair.

"They drank, they watched TV, played video games, or gambled—there's a million ways to do it. But some fought their way out. Million ways to do that, too."

Jack dropped his eyes. They latched onto the high-heeled boots over on the side of the room. The high polish made him think of Sijohn's little-Napoleon strut through the yard. He thought how the coach dressed better than the other teachers, how all his suits "came in three pieces".

"I'm not saying you're a quitter. In fact, you hang on, you survive."Sijohn leaned forward, eyes boring in. The cushion squeaked, bringing Jack to attention.

"I'm giving you an opportunity. Nobody gave me one. Don't just throw it away. Ask yourself, 'Who is Jack? What does Jack want?' Tell me that!"

Sijohn's body stiffened up, as if punctured by a thumbtack someone had left in deep leather. This time the dismissal was plain enough. The godfather whisper vanished.

"Get out of here...before I lose my temper with you, too."

Jack wasted no time getting back to the court. Jared had already switched to the gold of the second team, the razor necklace less conspicuous against yellow. He glared at the blue of Jack's shirt.

When Jack got to school the next day, his face was all over campus. The paper was out. The inside joke he'd shared with Martinez had gone outdoors. There he was snapping his wrist down after that last free-throw. One stranger came up and said:

"Well...are you ever going to miss?"

How do you answer that? At least he was being noticed. That wasn't bad if you had nothing to hide—which was true until math class. He was just a tad late, but late he was.

Jack fell for the old ostrich trick—Chambers camouflaged against the desk by sticking her head in her purse. Jack slunk in. The teacher's olfactory organ picked up odor of boy on the sly. After Jack sat down, she came out of the purse and said very politely:

"Mr. Marston, I see your picture is in the newspaper. Please stand up."

The paper was flapped out for the rest of the students to see. There was Jack, very serious, shooting that seventy fifth free-throw that didn't count at all. The class ate it up, waiting for the put-down sure to come.

Jack stood up, head down.

"Might I rephrase this caption. The question is not when you'll miss, but rather, when you'll be on time?"

The class guffawed. The humiliation of a celebrity was more fun than any ordinary humiliation. The math teacher glowed at her own cleverness. The laughter was strong enough deterrent for tardiness—a referral didn't follow.

Annie didn't laugh, but she did smile. Jack realized this really wasn't humiliation at all. Chambers' wasn't mean spirited. She wouldn't pick on somebody weak. In a way, she was honoring him.

The reaction at practice was also good-natured. Dereck challenged him to a free-throw contest, a joke in itself. The center was a fifty percenter in games, only slightly better in practice. Jack declined, saying Dereck was too good for him. The challenger strode off, telling anyone who'd listen:

"Hear that? Marston's not in my league!"

Finally, he said it once too often and Jared added, "Yeah—little league."

CHAPTER 28

JACK TALKED JAMAL into walking over to
Annie's with him. For once, Jack's bike was going to
stay at home. He really didn't know what to expect at
the party. Maybe Jamal was nervous, too. Tara would
be there—in fact, that's why Jamal got an invitation.

Neither talked for a few blocks. Jack showed Jamal
the shortcut through the farm trail. As they emerged
back to the street, he tried to think of something to say.
With Annie's house just around the corner, Jack finally
thought of what Sijohn said about fighting. He said to
his friend:

"You're a born fighter."

"Are you kidding? At my size?"

"Then why always fight?"

"I don't."

"When don't you fight?"

Jamal looked around, as if telling a secret. "When
there's no crowd."

Jack shook his head, not understanding.

Jamal said, "I wait for a crowd."

"Why?"

"To break it up."

Jack shook his head again.

Annie's house came into view and they stopped talking. The boys knocked on the front door, but the living room appeared empty. Music came from the backyard. They followed the trail of sound. The stereo blared from a cement patio. A circle of boys surrounded box-like speakers. No girls in sight.

The newcomers attached to the back of the circle. Jared was seated in the middle, holding court like King Arthur at the Round Table. Moe, Ryan, Eric, and Dereck stood with their backs to Jack and Jamal. Jared saw them, though, and interrupted Dereck in the middle of a story.

"Well...look who's here."

Jared flipped a hand, and the circle opened slightly for Jack to enter. Even though he had taken Jared's job away, Jack was not excluded from the circle. Somehow, the invitation seemed exclusive. Unless Jared counted, Jamal was the only second stringer at the party—the seventh out of seven boys. He lingered on the periphery like an unwanted child, as if rank on the team prevented full acceptance.

Using that logic, of course, Jared belonged out with Jamal. Jack wasn't about to suggest that. He took a step forward. His friend was left behind, an outsider.

"How do you like this place?" Jared asked. He made

it sound like he was the owner. "Seen the pool?"

The music stopped. The captain started to get up when feminine voices set him down again. The girls deployed into their own tight little circle, about ten feet away.

Someone had counted right: seven boys, seven girls. The soccer party had been for the entire team. This party was for the elite. The arithmetic was accurate—Chambers would be proud.

The girls wore pants that stuck to legs like second skin. Annie's color was peach. It was topped by a flowery blouse and cinched by a belt. The dark honey-colored hair brushed by her face with a sweep. Her nails had a fresh coat of color to match her pants.

Tara was first to break the female clique. Jamal, the outsider, was rescued from the closed circle of boys. He was led to the boombox. A song selected and the air was filled with sound. Drums and guitar spit a staccato beat into the yard. The decibel level for talking soared into yelling range. Jack felt a tap on his shoulder.

Annie said, "Dance with me?"

Jack's mouth opened. No words came out.

Jared answered for him. "Go for it."

Everyone laughed. It was fast music and couples weren't touching. Annie waited for Jack to start, but too many eyes were on his back and dancing was something he didn't know how to do. When there was more dancers on the floor, he joined them on the patio

Jack wobbled his feet in an uncertain shuffle. His partner did likewise, but with confidence. Annie was unrestrained, lost in her own movement. Her eyes focused somewhere above his head, not seeming to notice Jack imitating her step. Still, he was glad when the music ended. His voice sounding loud in the gap between tracks.

"I'm not good at this."

"Easy to fix. It's my party."

She went back to the disc player. The driving beat of the next song stopped. The boys booed. A slow song began. The male attitude reversed.

"All right!"said Ryan

Girls cozied against boys, slowly swaying to music. No one was left out, no wallflowers. Everyone was matched with a date. Jared's hands fell against Grace's waist and they floated to a corner. Jamal nuzzled against Tara, small hands attaching to small shoulders. Annie came back from the stereo to Jack.

They were face-to-face but motionless, hands down. The other dancers floated like satellites around them. From the corner, keeping an eye on things, Jared spied the non-dancers.

"Well..."he said with a comic impatience, "get with the program."

Annie giggled. Jack forced a smile. He raised his left hand formally, according to rules of dance. A small, soft hand went onto it. Her other one nestled down on his shoulder automatically, like it belonged there.

He became just like the other boys in the open air, except his girl felt softer against his chest, smelled sweeter against his cheek. He maneuvered away from the pack of dancers so they'd have some breathing space. Annie pushed from him a little bit.

"I'd better stay close. My parents aren't home."

"Who's here then?"Someone was lurking in the house.

"That's my aunt. My dad sells drugs. He's in Vegas."

Jack stopped dancing. His eyes bugged.

Annie laughed and said, "The pharmaceutical kind."

Jack's eyes did not sufficiently debug.

Annie laughed again. "The legal kind."

Her head went back to his chest, but inward toward his face instead of outward toward the party. As she turned, her chin gently brushed his shoulder. He felt an eyelash blink shut against his neck. A long, lush song of love began to play.

CHAPTER 29

THE BOYS AND girls split along sexual lines when the music ended. Each returned to respective headquarters. The females moved back into the house. The males regrouped around the mute CD player.

The distinction became less subtle between Jack and Jamal. Both were on the team. Both had cheerleader girlfriends. But Jack was first string and Jamal wasn't. The shorter man was again squeezed out.

Jamal gazed back at the house for another rescue from Tara. None came this time. He was forgotten as the boys began to tease each other, this time about girlfriends instead of sports. Words whipped around like locker room banter. The ice was broken.

"Doin' all right!" Dereck said to Jared, extending his hand for a shake. The captain let the hand hang there.

"A little kiss," Jared said, "and the boy goes crazy."

"Douse him," said Eric. "The big man's hot!"

Ryan made a shivery pass over Dereck's head with

some ice. An ice cube escaped and cooled his head off. "Cut it out,"Dereck bellowed. He swept his hair with a large hand. The ice flicked out. He discovered the rest of his mane dry enough. Somewhat appeased, he said, "You guys are just jealous."

A barrage of laughter met that accusation. Jared stole a pencil out of Dereck's pocket.

"Doin' a little homework?"

Dereck tried to grab it back, but Jared squeezed it tight.

The mild confrontation was serious enough to evaporate conversation. Finally Dereck confessed sheepishly:

"For phone numbers, Stupid."

The captains face darkened. He shot back, "You couldn't get your mother's phone number."

The laughter burned Dereck's face. He made another stab for the pencil – it wasn't a joke to him – but Jared wrenched it away. Holding off Dereck with a scowl, the captain unbutton his shirt. He brandished the razor blade between two fingers.

"Who you callin' stupid?"

Dereck didn't answer. Jamal slipped away and went toward the house unnoticed.

Jared glared at the center, then dropped the blade like a guillotine into the wood pencil. It split without a crunch. The eraser end decapitated coldly and cleanly. The useless rubber top bounced on the cement like a lifeless head.

Dereck didn't move but didn't like it.

Jared waved the leaded end like a mutilated trophy. "Take it," he said, iron in his voice.

Dereck still didn't moved.

"I said take it." The order was unmistakable.

The captain—pencil in one hand, blade in the other—wound to his feet. Dereck stepped away, lowering into a semi-crouch. The circle expanded to give them room. No one else moved or said anything.

The screen door slammed. Tara was first out, with Jamal at her side. Then other girls infiltrated, each capturing the arm of a former dance partner. Jared threw the pencil down, refusing Grace's hand. His face was tight, his body ready to strike.

Dereck crouched lower, holding his ground.

The captain covered the pencil with the heel of his shoe. He ground it into graphite dust. With Grace restraining his arm, he kicked the remnants of lead away as so much trash.

It was over. Dereck straightened up. Jared put the gold jewelry back around his neck. The center stalked off with his girl. Jack felt Annie latch on to his arm. She pulled him away from the others and down some steps. Evidently she had forgotten the rule about staying with the rest of the party.

Soon they were by a blue, iridescent pool. And alone for the first time. She kicked a sandal off and rolled the pants up her calf. She sat on the pool ledge, glimpsed at Jack, then immersed the naked leg into liquid blue.

"Cold," she said.

Soon Jack was next to her. His shoes came off in record time and yes the water was cold. Her toes waved in the self-induced current. The toe nails were peach like her fingers. She gave him an unintentional underwater nuzzle. The weightlessness made the touch playful, not serious. He returned it, intentionally. He searched for something to say.

"Where's your mom?"

"With Daddy. Momma loves to travel. She likes being a wife more than a mother."

Wrong question, Jack thought. He coughed.

"She and Daddy have these big secrets. They always lock their door and talk." She looked up at Jack and then down. "I'm the only one outside."

"I'm sorry."

"That's what love is—sharing things. Someday I'll have someone to trust..." She looked up at him again. "...and someone who trusts me. Someone who will always have my back."

Annie decided to be brave. The other sandal came off. She dipped the dry leg in the pool, lowering it with a shiver.

"Then I'll make my own secrets..." She stopped. The already wet leg came out and touched against Jack for warmth. "I just need somebody to tell them to."

Not having any secrets handy, Jack didn't know what to say. He thought about putting his arm around her waist. Somehow it seemed bolder because they weren't dancing. His plan of action was halted by a sober question.

"What was that all about?"

He stared into the crystalline water, wanting to phrase this right without criticizing Jared.

"Couple of starters had an argument."

"You're a starter."

Jack didn't answer. His eyes dodged up to the roof overhang. Black solar panels stared back at him like false mirrors.

"You can trust me." Her foot traced a slow figure eight through the water.

Jack relaxed his own legs. They floated down in slow motion, scraping softly against the side of the pool. He squinted at them through the water. His face wavered back like a reflection in a shimmering batch of jello.

Some slow music finally broke the silence, wafting down the steps like an invitation. Annie got up and shook her legs off. Jack did the same. The air hit their sensitized calves like a blast from a frigid blow dryer.

Annie said, "I'm cold."

He wanted to hold her. He thought about the music and put out his left hand as if to dance.

She ignored the hand. Both arms swung around his neck instead.

His left hand had nowhere to go but down again. It fell to the side of her waist and stopped.

He felt the long nails press lightly against his neck.

His arms continued around her back, clasping tightly. Their stomachs touched.

He thought about kissing her, like Dereck had done with his girl. He wondered what she'd do. The music died.

She turned her face toward his.

He hesitated. The moment passed.

"We'd better go up," she said after a second.

He touched her hand on the way up the stairs. Her fist tightened on a finger. The four wet feet mixed water footprints together up the steps. Annie released his finger when the others came into view.

"Some hostess I am," she murmured. "The girls must be wondering where I went."

"I won't tell," Jack assured.

"That's OK..." She smiled at him. "You can tell." The smile twisted at the corners. "I'm going to."

She disappeared into the squadron of girls. The boys were again abandoned by the opposite sex. They girdled tightly around in a circle to exchange gossip. Jared was in the middle, of course, and Jamal lingered on the outside. Everyone but the big center knew his place. Dereck was part way in and part way out of the circle.

The big man took a reluctant step closer. It was better to belong than not to belong. The circle absorbed him inside and grew larger, like an amoeba taking in nourishment. The in-group opened again when Jack neared. The newest first stringer took his place inside.

On the way home, Jack said to Jamal, "Lucky that fight broke up."

Jamal looked sideways, wondering if everyone knew he brought the girls back outside. "When you're little, you can get killed."

"Neither one was little."

"One had a weapon...and knew how to use it. The other guy was big."

"You've never been..."

"Razors can kill you. And a big guy gets you on the ground. He starts kicking. You're history."

They walked some more. Jack said, "You can lose a tooth that way."

Jamal smiled wide enough to let the gap peek out the side of his mouth. Jack said, "People think you never back away."

"You pick your spot."

"A spot?"

"A spot where you have a chance. A spot where everyone's watching. You get a rep..."

"For what?"

"For not giving up," Jamal said. "People can't resist someone who won't give up." He beamed the gap-toothed grin. "They don't know what to make of it."

"Especially from a little guy," Jack said.

"Or a skinny one."

Jack said, "Ouch."

CHAPTER 30

JACK WAS ON a high, sweeping into the next week like a new man. The big news after Monday's practice was that the Mountaineers had been trounced. They had been out pushed, out rebounded, and outscored. There was only one undefeated team now.

With two games to go, Kennedy would play the Eagles and then Ventura. The first was an away game, which might mean riding with the beloved Mrs. Dodd Jared seemed to be looking forward to that encounter. It was a long trip, up near Grant's college.

Everyone treated Jack like a first stringer at practice. The ball was passed to his side more often. Jared was aggressive on defense, but the rough stuff disappeared. Just as Sijohn expected, Jack was earning his way to the starting five.

He seemed to have a spot reserved on the picnic bench after practice, too. After Annie's party, everyone assumed he had a girlfriend. No more security blanket dragged over to foreign territory. Jack would have been missed if he wasn't there.

The last practice before the Eagles game sent the exhausted boys away in a faintly optimistic mood. If they could redeem themselves, Sijohn would slacken the agonizing workouts. Annie wasn't at her usual space on the picnic bench afterwards. He finally saw her coming out of the girls' showers. Her face was scrubbed clean and her hair still wet. When he was close enough, she said:

"Walk me home?"

Jack locked his bike and met her back at the picnic table. Sijohn came out of the gym and marched by. He seemed to scrutinize Annie, perhaps looking for pink lipstick. He nodded at Jack with a faint smile and went by. When they were out on the street, Annie said:

"We have a friend in common."

"Who?"

"Power of the media..."hinted Annie

"Nothing can stop it,"Jack said.

"The journalism teacher said it once." Annie giggled. "Darrin took it to heart."

Jack thought of holding Annie's hand again, maybe at the corner when they changed directions.

Playfully, Annie said, "He looks at me like he's in a dream."

"Huh?" Jack didn't get it.

"Darrin,"Annie said. "He looks at me when he thinks I'm not looking."

"Huh?" Jack still didn't get it.

"He looks at me like you do."

"Oh,"Jack said. He got it.

"Not to change the subject..." Annie said. "but that fight with Jared..."

Jack hesitated. Jared was her friend.

"I've heard different stories."

The corner came. Jack captured her hand.

"Fighting's stupid,"Annie said. She squeezed his hand. "Use your head—that's what God gave it to you for."

Jack thought, "Easy for a girl to say." He squeezed her hand back.

The time to meet the Eagles finally did arrive. Sijohn took his own car to the game. A bright yellow bus pulled up for the players. Jack, with nothing better to do, examined the driver.

It was a woman. A cap was clipped to the hair like she was a waitress in a greasy diner. She was thin. Her body had the musculature of a grasshopper. She was serious. Arms were carefully placed on the steering wheel at ten to two. Her upper trunk leaned forward with exactness. She was tired, but maybe just with life. Her numbed expression reminded Jack of his mother at the tail end of a double shift.

It was Jared's favorite driver.

Mrs. Dodd watched them board. She looked at them as if they should all be quarantined. The skin stretched tight across her face when Jared stepped up. He dragged an overstuffed bag behind him. When he reached the top step, Mrs. Dodd straight-armed him to a stop like a traffic cop.

"No trouble from you, young man."

The former imitator put a hand to his chest as if to say, "Who...me?"

She let him by. He enthroned himself in the back of the bus. Hs legs made a "V"wide enough for two boys.

Jack was last to board, on purpose. He wasn't quite sure where to go. Did he belong in the front with second stringers? Or in the back with starters? He lingered at the top of the stairs.

Jared straddled the back center row like he owned it. His feet stretched down the aisle. Jack looked for an invitation to wedge into the pack. None came.

Fortunately, Jamal had a place saved for him right next to the driver. Jack dropped into it. What did he expect? This wasn't Annie's party. He didn't have a cheerleader on his arm now. There were dues yet to be paid.

The bus ride was picture perfect, at least from Mrs. Dodd's vantage point. Pre-game nervousness put a lid on horseplay. The boys weren't even rowdy at the railroad tracks, when the bus cut its engine. There'd be time for yelling on the way home—if they won.

And that didn't turn out to be a problem. The Eagles game was Jack's best yet. He scored twelve points in the first half alone. Five of them were free-throws. The string of swishes stayed alive.

By the third quarter, the outcome of the game wasn't in question. Jack hit the bench and stayed there. Jared took the floor with the second string to dredge out the garbage points. The only excitement in the fourth quarter was created by fans. Screams erupted behind the visitor's bench. Nothing was happening on the court, so the players all turned around. They were just in time to see a wicked left hook connect. A straight right cross brought an "ooh"from the crowd. It put a boy down.

The game went on below but nobody watched. Finally, the combatants were separated and order somewhat restored. Before Jack turned around, he noticed Kennedy had an extra fan. A figure in a black leather jacket joined the top row, visitor's side.

It was none other than Grant, laundry sack hauled over shoulder like he was going home. He had come to see if little brother was any good. His mother was right—life wasn't fair. First string or not, Jack was collecting splinters during the one game Grant attended.

A surge went through the crowd as another fight broke out. The Eagles weren't use to losing, or at least their fans weren't. Jack was happy to escape to the lockers at the final buzzer. He snuck a look at the top row on the way out. Grant wasn't there. Jack thought, he's happy I'm on the bench.

The win restored everyone's spirits. All the hard practice had paid off. Ryan and Eric snapped their towels at the first naked bodies to test the showers. Dan stuck his head in before the nonsense got out of hand.

"Out and ready in five minutes,"he bellowed. "Coach says no showers... too many fights 'round here..."The boys turned their wrath on the manager. Dan dodged a towel from one of the boys, then tried to reason with the mob:

"Gotta get out of here before more fights."

A chorus of boos met that argument. The manager waited out, then responded with a new angle:

"Mrs. Dodd says..."

More boos, but this time at the bus driver. Dan grinned, happy to deflect anger onto a scapegoat.

"She'd just as soon leave you for the Vultures..."

Another chorus of boos.

"...I mean Eagles,"the manager corrected.

Ryan rifled another towel at the retreating Dan.

Sweat suits were dragged back over sweaty bodies. Before they went out the door, Jared yelled, "Starters meet at my locker."Jack was first.

"What's up?"he asked.

"Just wait,"Jared said.

When the rest of the starters arrived, he slid a towel off the backpack. Jared slowly pulled a baggy out of his satchel. The boys gathered in a semicircle, present.

Dereck whistled. "What's that... is it what I think it is?"

"What do you think, I wouldn't have the real stuff? I stole it from my older brother. And we share it with Mrs. Dodd tonight,"sneered Jared.

Jack shifted uncomfortably and said, "What do you mean?"

Jared looked at him like he had volunteered for duty. In fact, everyone looked at Jack. Jared said:

"You stick the baggy in Odd Dodd's bag where she

keeps her smokes. We call the cops and the old bag gets arrested."

"She will lose her job and she's done nothing wrong,"Jack said in astonishment.

Jared eyed Jack and snarled each word, "I got suspended from school and the team. That Odd Dodd deserves everything that's coming to her."

Jared high fived Ryan and Eric.

"You won't get caught and she will get busted," Jared's eyes blazed and in a low, deep growl he said, "No one ever messes with me, I always get even. Always."

CHAPTER 31

JARED HELD THE baggy up for admiration, then reburied it in Jack's bag. A shadow of triumph crossed his face when Jack didn't object.

Ryan said, "She doesn't know you're a starter now."

Then Eric: "You'd sit in the back with us from now on."

"We'd better hurry,"Jared said, "or the old lady'll leave us."

Five choice seats were still empty in the back when they got to the bus. The reserves knew better than to sit there. Jack sat next to Jamal again—his seat was still there, too. By leaning forward, he was almost close enough to touch Mrs. Dodd.

It would have been usual, of course, to celebrate the victory on the way home. But the quiet in the rear of the bus set the volume for the rest of the team. They were the leaders.

The bus lurched off into the evening air. Jack

fingered the plumb baggy in his carrying bag and placed it in his hand. He was surrounded by people and suddenly felt alone. He didn't belong in the back with the others. Tonight could change all that.

He put a hand in a sweatsuit pocket. He felt the baggy with damp fingers. The inside lights in the bus went off. He stared at the driver's back, then past her through the window. *She was giving me every opportunity.*

Mrs. Dodd's reflection looked back at him off the windshield. That face, the skinny tight face with the waitress cap, penetrated his mind. He remembered Jared teasing her before the suspension, her face purpling up with rage. He imagined the expression when the police found marijuana in her bag. She would not be allowed to drive for the school system again.

Great fun that'd be. He pictured the pandemonium, the faces of his teammates enjoying the chaos. The baggy crinkled inside his fist. The bus rolled to a stop at the railroad tracks. Jared crept up to the front. He whispered so just Jack could hear.

"What're you waiting for? We'll be at school soon."

Mrs. Dodd spotted him and said harshly: "Get back to your seat."

"Yes Ma'am,"he said politely. Jared, the perfect student, went back to his seat obediently. No one could pin this on him. Jack would be the one caught and suspended this time. Jared would be the first string again.

Jack reached down into his pocket and withdrew the plumb baggy. The back of the bus saw him do it. They stopped talking.

Grins danced across faces. They were ready for the prank... ready for zero hour. The bus started again, bumped over the tracks, gained speed down the throughway.

Sijohn had once complimented Jack's basketball instincts: the ability to make the right play at the right time. More was at stake now than a basketball game. What he did next had no reason behind it, as if feeling had taken over his body for an instant.

His hand took the dull, brown grass shinning in the clear, plastic baggy. Jack opened the bus window. The brownish pieces blew in the wind and almost looked like snowflakes dancing in the air. He did it on emotion more than thought. It was the right thing to do, no matter what anyone else thought.

Jack realized what went out the window with it. The chance to be first string. To really belong. He would never be with others now. No one would have his back or understand the reasons for his actions.

The sun was on its way to oblivion by the time they reached Kennedy. Blue clouds smoldered over a bright orange blaze of fire. Jack wished he could vanish like the sun. Instead, he had to hit the showers before going home. He mingled into the pack leaving the bus, trying to get lost. The second string didn't know what was up and Jack wasn't anxious to tell them.

The damp uniform was peeled off. He slogged through a cluster of starters on the way to the showers. Jared wasn't there. Disgust etched into team-mates' faces. Mouths shut and eyes averted like he was a bet they'd lost—a sure thing that finished out of the money.

The consensus was clear enough: Jack was a loser.

Jack got himself wet, sprayed a stream of soap from the dispenser, rinsed off. He hit dry land in record time. The silent treatment continued when he passed the other first stringers again. Jared still hadn't arrived to anchor the circle of scorn.

Jack flashed on the last soccer game of the season. There was silence then, too—silence that said more than words ever could. He had let them down again. He had been expected to carry this prank off.

Jack dressed fast enough to be first out and first to the bike racks. He unclicked his lock but didn't mount the bike. Instead he walked it toward the farm trail. Somehow the contact of dirt beneath his feet gave security, assured him the reality of earth and sky and gravity.

He couldn't wait to be alone out on the farm path. It was insulated from the school by a chain link fence crammed with bougainvilleas not in bloom. Night-sounds filtered through the bush as he got closer.

When he reached the trail, Jack began to run. The sun had made it down, maybe a minute before. Clouds dissipated over its exit, blue-black guardians of a fiery death. Night animals sent vague communications through the electric, orange afterglow. The bike rolled alongside Jack, slowing him down.

It was not a jog but a sprint, as if Jack was catching something, or escaping. The school disappeared, a distant memory. He could only hear footfalls, his own feet pounding loose, furrowed dirt. Gradually the pounding sucked into Jack's chest. Then the drumming reached into his ears, beat in his head, drowned out thought.

Jack came huffing around a tree, but then slowed abruptly to a trot. Somebody was standing in the trail ahead. He squinted into the waning light. The form was back-lit, the face indistinct. The body was solid and stocky as a fireplug. That was signature enough. It could only be one person.

Jack's legs unconsciously moved forward, like he was driven by a death wish in a nightmare. Details of identity sharpened into focus. Jared's game clothes showed under unzipped sweats. A blue tanktop was visible. A chain disappeared into it like a river of gold into jungle growth. When the two boys were close enough, Jared said:

"Still runnin'?" Then, with tiredness, as if he was the one out of breath: "Time you slowed down."

Jack's feet did just that. The drumming in his heart didn't. Jared waited a beat, then said more ominously:

"Marston, you just ran out of room."

The captain's feet widened over the middle of the trail. No one was going to move him out of the way, least of all this second stringer.

"It's time you stopped faking it,"Jared said.

Jack let his bike fall into the dirt.

Jared put a hand on his collarbone, found the golden chain draped over it, and gave it a tug. The razor flipped out onto the blue shirt. He ducked his head and removed the jewelry. He brandished the blade at Jack.

"I'm going to put this up your nose,"Jared said.

CHAPTER 32

MOONLIGHT GLINTED OFF the blade. If he had a death wish, Jared just might grant it.

Jack stepped back toward his fallen bike. The retreat was interpreted as a sign of weakness. The stocky legs moved forward. They planted wide over the middle of the trail.

"You've got to get by me," Jared said.

Jack weighed the possibility of a fight. It'd be his skinny legs against those muscular ones. It'd be his will against Jared's will. Jack wouldn't bet on himself. Nobody at Kennedy would.

Jack took another step back. The bike bumped his back leg. That was his ticket out, if he wanted it. Jared said matter of factly:

"You threw my property into the gutter."

Jack worked his feet into furrowed dirt, like a clean-up hitter digging in for a home run swing. Jared watched him, eyes sharp and bright with malice.

"You've gonna pay, Marston."

It would be fists against a razor. No crowd to break it up. No one to hear them on the farm trail. The story would be told later, at school—Jared's version of it, anyway. Who'd believe Jack, especially after chickening out on the bus? He'd been set up to bleed, set up to lose.

Jack picked his bike out of the dirt. He rolled it around the border of the road, making a wide arc around Jared.

The captain studied his opponent. He was ready for a trick, a surprise attack, a sucker punch.

Jack didn't even look at him. To stay beyond reach of the blade, he stepped completely off the road. When safely past, he mounted his bike. Jared didn't follow. He had won without even the risk of fighting.

The stocky boy's laughter hissed up from behind with a cold draft of air. It jangled Jack's nerve endings like a breeze skirling through a wind chime he didn't know was there. He pedaled harder, trying to escape from it, trying to escape from himself.

Suddenly Jack felt sick. Vomit burped into his mouth. The foul-tasting saliva was ejected in thick spittle. Some of it had to be swallowed back down. A smack of rankness wouldn't get off his tongue, like the taste of surrender.

Jack powered a thigh down on a pedal. Then he stood up on them, using his weight. His body shifted side to side, building maximum power toward home. The sound of laughter faded out.

Thoughts flowed in and out as each breath got harder, heavier. It would've been suicide to fight Jared. Why should he get pounded? The razor flashed in his mind, red with blood, his blood. Why should he risk getting cut?

The tires wedged into loose dirt, grinding through it like sand. Jack wrenched up on the handlebars. The bike jumped onto a tire track where heavy machinery had compacted the soil. Better to jump tread marks than be bogged down. The harder, bumpier path jolted through the bike frame, rattling a loose fender.

He couldn't get the confrontation out of his mind. Jared could have chased him. Everyone was always quite good about letting him run away. Grant always let him go, once Jack gave up. The hierarchy of power was preserved if all they saw was Jack's backside. Sijohn was right. Nothing would change if Jack didn't fight for it.

The trail turned uphill, solidifying over dried mud. He wrenched out of the tire track, wiggling the handlebars back and forth for extra power. He had to use all his weight to keep the same pace up the hill. His heart started to pound as the hill steepened.

In a game he might have stopped and signaled for a sub. He couldn't keep this up. But the game was over long ago, and Jack thrust on. He used the handgrips to counterbalance his weight over each pedal. He thought, I should have fought, even if it was suicide.

The trail went over a ridge and turned down. Like an ocean under a starless sky, nothing came back to assure the senses. Just emptiness, blackness. Bottoms

Up loomed ahead like an abstracted heaven, or hell. Jack accelerated with breathless ease.

There was no conscious decision to go for it...he was disgusted with all his decisions anyway. Thoughts ricocheted inside his skull without coming together to make sense. He had jumped the gorge before, but only as passenger, only with 500 cc's of power. He was on his own now, a solitary streak through night sky. There was no motor under him, no brother in front to squeeze for security. The eyes had to stay open. He had to take care of himself.

Two ramps lay ahead, abbreviated bridges over Bottoms Up. One was over the wide deep part, where his brother jumped the motorcycle. The other looked doable, over the narrow shallow end on the right.

He headed right, toward the neck, but didn't slow down. Every ounce of power was squeezed out of the bike. When he saw the plywood tramp, his rear hit the saddle again. This was all the speed he was going to get. Now he needed stability.

The bike bit into the ramp. The tires hummed over the plywood. Then the whirl of rubber stopped. Jack pushed down on a pedal. It didn't resist, as if a magic treadle that stopped time.

He sailed into another dimension, freed from earth and its trouble. The memory of pot gently rolling into a gutter blew away in the cool airborne breeze.

Jack kept his eyes open, forward to the ledge coming closer. The front wheel pulled up and the back wheel sank down. The bike tilted like it was going uphill, except nothing but air cushioned the tires.

The bicycle lost momentum and dropped in altitude. The ledge moved vertically, like an elevator going up slowly.

He slammed the wall, front tire first, maybe a foot from the top. Then the back tire hit, flattening against the cliff. The jolt was like jumping off a one-story roof. The handlebars twisted loose.

If this was Grant's motorcycle, they might have revved up and over onto flat land. But it was only a bicycle, and only Jack. He was jounced off the saddle. Head over heels, Jack lost his bearings.

Man and machine plummeted.

He didn't know the direction of the ground. He tried to get his feet pointed down, searching for a landmark like a diver lost in somersault. A flash of chrome came off his bike, but he didn't know if that was up or down.

All he needed was to land on his head.

CHAPTER 33

DIVERS CALL IT "getting lost." You kick out of a flip and reach out for the pool with your hands. Instead, you hit the water feet first.

Jack twisted and turned for what seemed like an eternity. He heard the bicycle clank down, off to the right. Then the eternity ended, fortunately with feet pointed down.

There was impact, then pain. Jack bottom-rolled in sandy soil, right ankle crunching in the dirt. He finally stopped face down, heart palpitating. The pit was soft with gravel and sand, like part of the trail.

That's what saved him. When his breathing got under control, he flipped right side up to survey damage. His toes wiggled obediently. He was alive, anyway.

Jack scanned the ditch wall. The black walls of the hole made it seem like peering from the wrong end of a telescope. He crouched to his feet, but toppled back down. The right foot didn't hold. He rolled up the sweat suit leg. The outside ankle bone was wide and flat as a fried egg. A cushion of blood puffed around the borders.

Jack looked up again at the sky. The orange haze of sunset had dimmed out completely. A charcoal canvas remained, periodically disturbed by blips of cumulus. The clouds were full black now, inky puffs of smoke. The North Star gleamed through like a beacon from a lighthouse warning him to go back.

He wished he could. The slope inclined enough to frustrate a climber—a two-legged climber at that. He followed the North Star down. The light glanced off an object on the other side of the gorge. He recognized the smudged chrome of handlebars. The metallic glimmer was dirty and dull, tinged with age and hopelessness. It was a racing bike, not a heavy cruiser like Jack's. Caliper brakes sprouted over the bars like electronic antennae.

Of course, Jack thought, Mark Lowe's bike.

Black smoke clouds swished overhead. More stars blinked through. Jack squinted at the pencil-pricks of light. He back focused his vision to scrutinize the ledge. A board from the ramp jagged over the pit, out of reach by more than a body length.

He gazed again at the starry sky, like it was a crystal ball and he was a fortune teller. His eyes narrowed—the dots of white light squiggled into confusion. God didn't solve problems by writing messages in the sky. It wasn't that easy.

He stopped trying to force sense into random stars. Mark Lowe's bike lay across from him, both wheels present. Most ten speeds had quick-release tires. Easier to fix flats, but also easier to steal wheels. Evidently, Bottoms Up was too steep for thieves. An idea, dim as junctions between stars, began to connect in his brain.

Standing up step one.

He expected the ankle to hurt and it did. By hopping on one foot, he managed to reach the ten speed bike. The tires were flat. Doesn't matter, Jack thought. They're not gonna roll, not straight up. No derailleur on the front to mess with, only a butterfly clip. He felt for the pin at the center. He pinched it, twisted it. The axle slid out. He removed the wheel from the fork of the bike frame.

On to step two.

Jack pulled his sleeves down so they covered his palms. The doubled cotton of the gym suit protected his hands like a pot holder. He seized a handful of spokes in each padded mitt. Jack stretched the wires in opposite directions, away from each other. The spokes deformed so that a football-shaped hole gaped through the wires.

Go to step three.

Jack limped back over to the ramp. He positioned the tire so the hole was away from his hands. With an overhand swing, he flung the wheel up toward the ramp. The spokes busted against the 2 by 4 and bounced off. The next try had better aim. The wires caught on the stake, hooking onto it like a lopsided doughnut.. He tested it with body weight.

Ready for the final step, the only one that mattered.

Jack worked five deep breaths through his chest. He

adjusted the tire, taking hold of it with both hands. He tried his weight on it again. The wood did not budge. He slid the wheel along the board. When it bumped the wall, he tested it again. Still solid. The football-shaped groove clinched securely around the base of the ramp.

Using the wheel for support, he monkeyed up the vertical wall. Spokes jabbed him from the tire rim, penetrating the gym suit mittens, digging the sides of fingers. He did not let go. Jack ascended the Bottom Ups wall like a boy on a jungle gym. He climbed, he scrambled, he lurched.

Finally, a toe bumped wood. When both legs got there, he scissored them up over the board, crossing ankles to lock on. Freed from the burden of primary support, his hands climbed up the wheel. When he was high enough, he let go of rubber and grabbed for wood. Then he bellied over the 2 by 4.

From there it was easy. Arching his back like a caterpillar, Jack wiggled the length of timber. Weeds had sprouted around and under the platform. He flopped into the cushion of vegetation. The coldness of the earth seeped into his back to remind him it wasn't over yet.

Get up, he thought. Get home.

He rose to all fours, to knees alone, then to one leg. The injured foot touched down. The ankle protested with another spasm of pain. He hopped to adjust balance, then tried the bad foot again. This time he was ready for it. Half walking, half hopping, he shoved off for home. Nobody'd be there—his mother was working a double shift. It only took a few steps before he decided school was closer—home was over a mile away.

Jack started hobbling back to Kennedy. Another eternity went by. Then his heart gave a leap—light was ahead. There'd be help. Still, it would be embarrassing. Chickening out on the bus, falling into a hole.... He shivered at what Jared would say.

He passed bougainvilleas, bike racks, the car lot. No flowers in bloom, no bikes in racks, one car in the lot. He rounded a corner and saw the gym door open. A leaky shower wept into the night. There was a glow of tube lights. He skipped to a locker, grabbed it, rattled it. A voice echoed out of the office:

"Whatsamatter?"

Jack didn't answer.

"Who's there?"the voice commanded.

It was Sijohn.

Jack tried to walk into the PE office with a semblance of normal stride. The coach was enveloped, as usual, in his soft leather throne. Cold florescent light, reflected off the round face, making him look faintly luminous, like a moon.

"I had an accident,"Jack said.

The medical routine followed. The fried egg ankle was inspected. Yes, Jack said, it hurt. The coach said parents would have to be called. Jack gave out his home number, knowing his mother wouldn't be there.

It came as a surprise when Grant answered.

CHAPTER 34

SIJOHN KEPT IT short, put the phone down. He rolled the chair back, sinking down a couple of millimeters. His short stubby hand, nails manicured and polished, tapped across the desk.

"Tell me again what happened."

Jack told the story he had practiced on the long trek back to school. He had "fallen" into the ravine. Maybe it was the way Jack told it—a dart of a brow, a sideways glance to see if the story's being bought. All the words came out in the right order, but when he was finished Sijohn said:

"One more game and you had to do this?"

Jack glanced down, then up. He didn't answer.

The coach said suspiciously, "You weren't alone, were you?"

Jack's "Yes"was too firm, too quick.

"Who's bullying you around this time?" The coach wrapped his eyes around the skinny frame like a bear hug.

Jack's focus slipped off the luminous round face. The truth was oozing out with each second of silence. There would be no credibility in another denial.

"It was Jared, wasn't it?"

Jack didn't respond.

The tube light illumined a bead of perspiration in the gray crewcut. The manicured hand slapped at it like it was a mosquito, felt only moisture, and dropped onto the desk again. The coach hunched forward in the chair.

"Want me to handle it for you?"

"No," Jack said, not even considering it. He couldn't go running to Mommy or Coach. That would be mixing apples and oranges, kids and adults. He had to handle this himself.

"Find your own way then." His eyes descended Jack's neck, surveying the skinny body. "Maybe not with fists...but somehow." There was a rap on the outside gym door.

Jack shifted uncomfortably. Another knock, louder, bammed on the door. The coach swatted his wrist through the air at the noise, like it was another insect to be done away with.

"People have to know you want it...want it more than they do."

Still another boom, this time closer. Someone pounded a locker—the crash had a metallic aftershock. The coach lost his concentration, seeming to examine something across the room, or deep inside. He looked suddenly tired, burnt out. The manicured, stubby hand retracted across the desk and folded into the other one.

Grant didn't have to knock anymore. He was visible, standing just outside the office door. Sijohn's eyes refocused, face coming back to life. Tired of waiting, Grant entered without being beckoned. The presence of his brother made him shift into a passive mode. Jack slipped into the familiar second banana status he had within the family.

Grant's leather jacket wrinkled where a sleeve intersected a shoulder, stressing the bulk of muscle beneath. The Mutt and Jeff contrast was accented by the coat hanger shoulders holding up Jack's tank top uniform.

The coach didn't comment on that, didn't seem to notice the disparity between brothers. The patient's condition was given, business-like, and both Marstons were dismissed out of the office.

Jack made it outside, stepping lightly on the bad right foot. The clear unshaded lightbulb outside the door shone on the electric blue motorcycle.

Jack followed obediently, hopped on the back, grabbed hold. The engine roared. They were off, but not toward home. Jack yelled:

"Where we goin'?"

No answer came back with the wind. They bent into a turn, accelerated down a tree-lined street, made another turn. Jack knew the way by heart. The roads clicked into place like the automatic twists of a combination lock. The cycle burred to a stop under six stories of white stucco.

Jack didn't want to get off the bike. He wanted to go back to his own bed to recover in his own way. He didn't need any help, especially from strangers at a hospital. With a heavy breath, he touched his ankle. It throbbed. He lightened the weight on it.

Grant half-turned and said, "Coming or not?"Jack sighed, all the air releasing from his chest. He hobbled toward the double white doors, ready to be taken care of.

The stairs were the worst—no way to cheat weight over to the good foot. Grant was waiting at the door by the time Jack got to the top. The volunteer at the hospitality desk was young and pretty and blonde. When Jack limped in, she rose behind the desk.

The gesture moved Grant into action. Jack felt a beefy arm scoop under his thigh. Another beefy arm caught him under the shoulders. Jack was hoisted like an animated Greek statue. The muscles inside the leather jacket bulged. He froze for a moment, giving her time to exercise imagination. Jack thought, 'Maybe he doesn't know where to go.' He whispered up at his brother's face:

"Follow the blue line."

But the blonde said, "Emergency's downstairs."

Grant wavered for a moment, then decided for the audience at the end of the blue line. He pivoted to smile at the blonde, then was off. Jack was still airborne when the elevator door opened on his mother's floor.

Grant strode to center stage like an actor making an entrance. He stopped at the nurses' station.

A large woman was behind a counter, behind a desk, behind a lamp, finally behind glasses tinted pink. The helmet of ivory hair hovered face down, not seeing them on purpose.

It was Broomhead.

CHAPTER 35

A HEAD NURSE cannot ignore a poor waif carried in like a babe in arms. At least not for long. After all, it's a nurse's job to succor the needy, help the helpless, salve such poor victims of fate.

The large woman's spectacles tipped up. Her neck craned around obstacles piled on the counter. Jack jerked his head away—it was hardly a return in glory.

Grant swiveled to absorb the whole room, front to back. It wasn't help he was looking for—the stage wasn't set yet. Imprisoned by the hard muscles, little brother was modeled in front of the nurse like an unwanted gift. Embarrassed, Jack scattered his eyes over the physical minutiae of the nursing station.

Charts, filling trays, clamps, medical devices, unknown boxes of white equipment, all were positioned to block direct access to the boss. Even the desk was placed way back as an added shield against interruptions. Finally, his gaze reached the small eyes and stuck.

They looked pink through the tint, like an aggressive

rabbit's. They widened in recognition.

"Oh, it's you."

She made it sound like he was a dog taken to a people hospital by mistake. This was Sally's kin, the one who called her "Broomhead."

She rose out of the barriers constructed between herself and trouble. The oily sheen on her face glistened damp and transparent, just like melting ice.

"Sally,"she called out. "It's your boy."

No answer. He wiggled in his brother's arms.

Maybe Sally was making rounds. It was swing shift, nobody else around. With reluctance, Mrs. Brumhaus dislodged herself from her throne. Her job was to delegate authority, not to dive in and do something. She and trouble were getting too close.

The Head Nurse nudged aside a stack of folders and repositioned some kind of scope. The obstacles were divided until there was a direct eye-line through the clutter. To Grant she said:

"What's the matter with him?"

She could have addressed Jack. The misdirection made him feel like a hospital commodity, a nonperson. He twisted in Grant's arms. The bands of steel sagged a little, bending with the first signs of fatigue. Grant repositioned the load, adjusting muscles to different tension. Jack wiggled again.

The muscles clamped down harder than ever. Mrs. Brumhaus squinted at Grant, attempting to verify that this was a Marston, too. She didn't see the resemblance, shook her head, pointed to the counter.

"Put him here."

She said it like Jack was a piece of baloney. Grant didn't comply, although the load wasn't getting any lighter.

"Where's my mother, Mrs. Marston?"

The nurse called out, "Sally!" Then to the boys, as if complaining about some flunky worker goofing off: "I'd like to know that myself."Jack, with a view over Broomhead's shoulder, saw a door open at the end of the hall.

The Head Nurse sensed that Grant wasn't letting go of his catch. Reluctantly, she shuffled around the counter, rolled up Jack's gym suit leg, and inspected the fried egg ankle. Sijohn had already taped it. The nurse sniffed at the shoddy construction of the amateur bandage.

"This has been tended."

Jack kicked the ankle up. The pant leg draped back down to cover the wound. The nurse took it as a defiance. She shoved the leggings back up again and dug her index finger under the tape. Out of the corner of his eye, Jack saw his mother pad toward them from the end of the hall.

Broomhead suddenly pulled on the tape. The bandage came off with a rip. Jack yelled in spite of himself. He had expected it to come off little by little.

Broomhead smile slightly at the cry, as if the sound was a small victory. Mrs. Marston at the middle of the hall now, said in her itty-bitty professional voice:

"What's happened?"Mrs. Brumhaus didn't turn

around to acknowledge her. Instead, she dangled the bandage in front of Jack as if to say, "Don't mess with me, boy."

The adhesive had been strong. Leg hairs splayed in the sticky tape like a spider without an abdomen. The Head Nurse dropped the surgical dressing on the floor—it was somebody else's job to clean it up. She poked at the swelled-up ankle with her fingernail.

"I've seen worse,"she said. "You don't belong here. We don't treat such minor..." she paused, choosing the word carefully... "inconveniences."

Mrs. Marston was close now, almost at the counter. The stage was set. Grant preened in front of her, displaying the attraction imprisoned in his arms. The audience was in place, and Jack was the main act. Not acknowledging Sally's presence, Broomhead said to the boys:

"This isn't an emergency room. You belong downstairs."

His mother's chin came up. She said very softly, "Please..."

Broomhead turned for the first time to look at her subordinate, as if to verify what she'd heard.

Grant stopped rocking his brother back and forth.

Slightly louder, Mrs. Marston said, "They belong right here with me."Her chin stuck out a little.

"What did you say?"The words were snapped like whips.

Jack's mother coughed, long and raspy, like an engine with a bad battery cranking on a cold morning.

She looked at her oldest son, the savior.

She looked at Jack, the screw-up.

She looked at Broomhead, the boss. The Head Nurse slashed her eyes away from her employee.

The cough finally died, along with the itty-bitty voice. Mrs. Marston's chin thrust out, tilting her head back. When she spoke again it was with authority, just a wee bit softer than she'd say to Jack, "This is Saturday and you'd better get out of bed."

"This is my son," she said into the big oily face.

Jack stopped breathing.

"And he'll see the doctor now."

CHAPTER 36

BROOMHEAD WAS STARTLED. She squinted through pink spectacles. Sally put a hand on each boy's shoulder like a mother bear drawing in cubs. The Head Nurse said:

"You're disrupting the floor." The pink eyes switched to Jack like he was nonbiodegradable litter. "Get him downstairs."

Jack twisted again. This time the hard muscles softened. The biceps weakened and the prisoner was deposited onto cold floor. Jack sat on his butt, surprised at the sudden freedom. Grant was backpedaling toward the elevator.

The good deed was done. The rest was dirty work. Somebody else could work out the details. He jabbed at the panel of buttons on the wall. Broomhead looked at the fallen boy at her feet with undisguised disgust.

"Don't leave him here."

Grant gave a flourish of his arm that meant, "He's

your problem now."The light above the elevator lit up. The door trolleyed open. The leathered arm resaluted the audience. He vanished behind a silent slide of collapsible metal.

Jack climbed up, standing as tall as he could on the gimpy ankle. His mother retouched his shoulder, pulling him back behind her. It was her battle. Her fury had abated. She was thinking again. She said halfway between order and request:

"3B is empty, Mrs. Brumhaus. Jack can wait for me in there."

The Head Nurse said matter-of-factly, "I'm not going to wake the resident for this"—a wrathful pink eye fell on Jack---"for this sprained ankle."

Mrs. Marston faced off the boss, chin forward, eyes brave. She seemed to waver, retracting a step, retreating below the level of "can't go back". She wanted time to rethink this. Her head jerked to the side, a signal for Jack to get moving.

Jack stepped toward 3B like he was afraid of a bullet in the back. Although the light was off, the room was only half dark. Institutions didn't trust patients they couldn't see. His eyes hadn't adjusted when the door reopened.

It was his mother. She was alone, Jack released a heavy breath. Broomhead had put his nerves on edge, like someone pinching him hard and not letting go. His mother sat next to him on the bed. The light stayed off.

Experienced fingers scooted up both legs. She tested the swollen ankle like she was buying a cantaloupe at the store. The good ankle was pressed for comparison.

"She's probably right,"Mrs. Marston said. "Just a mild sprain... not swollen too much."

"I don't want to cause you trouble,"Jack said. He stood up. "I didn't want to come here, anyway. I'll just go home."

The gym suit was allowed to drape back down. She found her son's face in the semidark.

"You screamed at her, Mom. You'll lose your job."

His mother half-smiled in the darkness. "You think that was screaming? You know me better."

Jack thought of the Saturday morning voice. Indeed, full volume had not been reached.

The door swung open.

Broomhead stood under the archway like a mobile mountain. She slapped the wall in a couple of places, but kept her eyes on the family Marston. The switch was finally located. A shaft of light beamed from the bed fixture like a ray gun. The flood of white made everyone squint but Broomhead. She rocked back on ripple soled shoes with an edge of superiority.

"Sally,"she said, "I'm telling you for the last time." Her eyes lasered into Jack. "Get your boy out of here. And you get back to work."

Mrs. Marston got up from the bed obediently. She crooked her back like dipping under a nonexistent bunkbed. But then she straightened. Her gaze disappeared into the pink shields over Mrs. Brumhaus's face. His mother brushed by the Head Nurse and left the room.

She's going to make peace, Jack thought. She's got to

make a living. He reclined back on elbows. Broomhead flashed the pink glare to him. Then a smile fleshed out the thin lips, a smile of triumph. She had won. Jack had lost.

"Get off the bed,"Broomhead said. Jack rose off his elbows. He couldn't cause any more trouble for his mother. The door opened behind them.

"Stay right where you are."

The voice was back. It was not the paint-removal voice, but it made you check the walls.

His mother, carrying a purse, swung into the room. The Head Nurse's lips thinned again.

"What did you say to me?"

"I'm not saying anything. I'm submitting something."

"Your resignation?"

"Stop treating me like an idiot. I am just as educated as you and I am great at my job."

She dug a hand into her purse, scratching around on top. Nothing!

Then in the middle. No luck.Finally the hand hit bottom.She found it, something Jack had forgotten was there.

It was a fat, square-shaped, bent-up scrap of paper. Jack recognized it—only one paper could have been folded that many times.

It compressed in her fist like a hard flat stone. The rest of the purse dropped to the floor.

Jack leaned forward on the bed.

His mother grabbed her superior by the wrist, pulling Broomhead's open palm toward her. She slapped the wadded paper into it with an overhand motion. It was almost like socking somebody, it was done with such vehemence. Mrs. Marston announced on the way out of the room:

"I'm going to wake the resident now and then email my copy of that paper to hospital adminstration."

Jack listened for the sound of a voice. Broomhead's mouth closed about the time the door stopped swishing back and forth.

She looked at Jack, then at the paper in her hand. She started to unbend the folds, but it had been hard and tight for so long it was like untying a knot.

Finally Mrs. Brumhaus said absently, "What's this?"

An application,"Jack answered. It was his turn to smile.

"An application for your job."

CHAPTER 37

MR. MARTINEZ WAS at his desk a good thirty minutes before zero period. His feet were visible, anyway, propped up on the desk. The rest of his body was shielded by newspaper.

Jack let go of the door to announce himself. If the teacher wasn't reading essays, he was reading something else. The door slammed shut. The paper dipped. Two weak eyes peered over half-glasses.

"Hello, Star."

Jack gave his best humble look.

"Just reading about you."

It wasn't the Outlook, but the free throw-around paper his mother took home from the hospital. The teacher noted Jack's skepticism.

"It says you won't play in the last game." The eyes bounced over the semi glasses. "How you feeling ?" Jack rolled his cuff up and sock down. A puffy pillow of blue-black still cordoned around the ankle, but the color was changing. He inserted a finger like a dipstick into the joint. A protective cushion of blood depressed like a wet sponge.

It hurt a little, not much. Jack readjusted the sock and stood up. Not much pain. Maybe his mother was right—he was going to live. The instructor grew tired of waiting.

"Well?"

Jack shrugged.

Mr. Martinez seemed to accept Jack's reaction, and his eyes retreated behind the newspaper.

"Want the good news or the bad news?"

Jack shook his head.

The teacher's nose reentered the winged-out paper. "First the bad news. The league's made Ventura an afternoon game."

"Huh?"

"Too many fights in the stands last time."

"But classes aren't out."

"That's the whole idea. Cut down on rowdies. Want the good news?"

"Sure."

"A certain teacher's taking a little field trip to the gym."

"The principal will love that."

Martinez winked. "That's what tenure's all about, young man." He winked again. "This is for first place."

"A tie for first."

"Close enough." The teacher ruffled the paper. "Ventura's got a hot player..." The bespectacled eyes scanned the newsprint to catch a name.

"Sterling,"Jack said.

"Not the one who..."

..."scored the win in soccer."

Martinez whistled. "Out for revenge, hey?"

"Fat chance—I probably won't play."

"That's not the word going around school." The teacher peered over his glasses. "My students say you're first string."

Jack said nothing.

"Wasn't that the idea?"

"I guess,"Jack said.

"You guess?"

Jack finally said, "I just thought it'd be different. Besides, I'm injured."

"So it's all down the drain, just like that." There was some more waiting, then Martinez said: "I have first stringers in class, Jack. And a lot of second stringers. But you know the real shame?"

Jack shook his head no. The banter had turned to cross-examination.

"It's when someone's first string and doesn't know it." The teacher's voice thinned out with impatience so that it was tight and brittle. "Now, if you don't mind, I've got classes to prepare."

Jack was dismissed into the cold to wait for the bell

with the rest of the early birds. The students ruffled a bit at his presence. He gave the humble look he'd given Martinez.

Martinez didn't call on him when class began, didn't even look his way. Jack was out quick when the bell rang. At least there wouldn't be tension with Chambers.

On the way to class he caught a rear view of Annie. Her long hair pony tail bound and secured by a ribbon. Jared was with her, and was doing all the talking. Annie just shook her head at him. The long tail of hair whipped back and forth.

Jack was still benched at practice that day. But "benched"was not the right word. He put up shot after shot at the side basket. A lot of them swished, but he couldn't get his full body into the shots.

The coach strolled over just before the end of practice.

"Feeling better?"

Jack nodded eagerly.

"Foot tender?"

Jack shook his head the other way.

Sijohn nodded thoughtfully, then blew his whistle for final free throws. The first string attacked the ball bag. Jack, not feeling part of the team, contented himself with the remains. When the crowd dissipated, what was left was a smooth ball and Dan for a partner.

The team manager bounced them out like a ball machine, and Jack returned most of them by way of the hoop. But now like he had before, not like the day 75 went down in a row. The final count was 20 out of 25, which the coach duly noted. Not bad, but not as good as Jared's 22 of 25.

But this wasn't a game, Jack thought. I could beat him in a game. He sank back on the bench as the others funneled down the stairs to shower. He wasn't even the best at free throws anymore. In the midst of feeling sorry for himself, he didn't hear Annie come up from behind.

CHAPTER 38

"I JUST WANT you to know I think it's awful."

The butterflies had no chance to take off. The voice was gentle, so soft Jack wasn't startled at all. He wondered what she was talking about, though. He looked down at his foot.

"You know...about Jared and you."

Jared, Jack thought, it has to be about Jared. Aloud he said, "What's he got to do with me?"

"He says you hurt your foot running away..." She spoke with slow embarrassment... "running away-from him."

Jack had let people think it was sprained in a game. Now with this other story... Besides, Jared could talk Annie into anything—she had said so herself. He had talked her into having the party. He could talk her into hating Jack.

"What else does he say?" His voice was stripped of passion or anger, just matter-of-fact like a telephone operator.

"That you never were first string. You just took his place for a while."

The pony tail shook as if to contradict the words. Her eyes glazed over with sympathy before wandering away over empty stands. All Annie wanted was a bond between them...a bond of sharing and truth. The dark honey eyes came back to him with more soft words.

"People don't know you, Jack. They'll believe what Jared tells them." Her eyes lit out on another journey.

"And you?"Jack asked.

"Something happened between you two..."

Jack picked up a basketball and let it go. He watched it bounce to the floor. His eyes didn't come up with the ball.

Annie waited.

Jack's eyes stayed on the floor. He was sick of Jared, sick of his own lying. But Annie'd never like him if she knew the truth. The honey eyes were on him when he finally looked up.

"If you don't trust me,"Annie said, "I can't help." She backpedaled away, reluctant to turn her back for a final goodbye. After eight reversed steps, she stopped and slid purse over shoulder.

"I don't understand you. I thought I did...once."

She finally turned her back on Jack, accelerating like she was late for something. He watched her turn the corner. The frustration in her voice stayed with him that night. He felt very alone. No one ever had his back.

The next day the yard didn't ruffle at his presence in quite the same way. The difference was subtle but real. He was noticed, but respect had changed to observation. Jack didn't bother Martinez before zero period. Martinez didn't bother him during Spanish. He glimpsed Annie between periods. She was with Darrin this time.

Jack got his share of attention when he walked into first period. Annie looked, but didn't see on purpose. She focused on his ribs, like he was blocking something of interest on the other side.

Practice was a last refuge. Jack watched from row one of the bleachers. The first team was practicing a "box and one"defense, with Jared the designated defender. The captain guarded Jamal man-to-man, while the others sank back into a zone.

"Keep Jamal from the ball,"Sijohn instructed Jared. "Don't worry about the drive...Ryan and Eric'll pick him up."

When the scrimmage started, tiny Jamal slipped in and out of the zone. Jared tried to follow but was too big and rubbed into Ryan. The whistle blared before Jamal's lay in had broken net.

"Pick him up,"Sijohn blared. Sterling will kill you on that. My God, the game's tomorrow. Don't you know that?"

Jack recognized the "Psych." A little fear would make them play better. From Jack's point of view, this wasn't necessary. Sterling had squashed in Jack's dreams all year.

"Teamwork!"the coach yelled, blowing his whistle.

"You can't win alone, but together you can. Help each other out."

Jared was all over Jamal when the ball came in. The little man feinted a drive, then pulled up short for a jumper. Jared timed his leap perfectly. The shot was rejected toward the stands, right into Jack's lap.

The captain came over to retrieve it. Jack got up to toss it halfway out, but Jared kept coming even after the ball was in his hands. He didn't stop until his face was in Jack's. It was their first contact since that night on the trail. The stocky boy enunciated so just his understudy could hear.

"Back on the bench, creep."He spat onto the wood floor. "You're not needed anymore."

Jack couldn't think what to say back. Words weren't going to be enough, anyway.

His mother was behind a newspaper when he got home that evening. She had been in her own private limbo ever since the confrontation with Broomhead. He asked for news on the job application. All he got was, "Any day...any day."She wasn't getting on with her life until there was an answer.

The last game day started out like any other. Jack kept the butterflies around, reminding himself that playing time was unlikely. He was getting used to his altered status at school. People watched him like an oddity. Conversations were always just below his level of hearing, at least until first period.

First thing Jack noticed was that Chambers wasn't at her desk. Then he checked out the first row. Annie, decked out in cheerleading costume, still ignored him.

She stared straight ahead, not even talking to Tara. It occurred to Jack that she was ignoring more than him. A silence descended on the rest of the class like a cold blanket of air. Something was going on.

He dropped his books and walked over to sharpen a pencil. Faces turned like he had tripped a silent signal on a burglar alarm. A distorted helium voice piped from the middle of the room—Jack wasn't sure where.

"Glad you could make it, Marston. Thought you ran away again."

The sound was pinched and squeaky, like chipmunks on a Christmas album. The roomful of people laughed. Fluid rose up Jack's chest and entered his windpipe.

"C'mon, Jack,"the voice twanged. "Tell us again how you sprained your ankle."

Jack tried to answer, coughing first to clear out the phlegm.

"Thataboy,"the voice interjected. "Choke for us."

Annie jumped to her feet. She looked at the class, then at Jack, then back to the class. The ponytail whipped her neck as she faced Jack again.

"Do something!"she blurted.

Before Jack could answer, her hair swished again and she bolted from the room.

CHAPTER 39

I GOT TO talk to her, Jack thought. But he didn't know what he'd say.

The eyes of his classmates glued to his back. He slid into the hallway. The last bell had cleared out the people. He walked by the VP's office, then through the big double doors.

No one in sight.

Where would she go? He thought of a student's last bastion of privacy. He reentered the building. The door marked "Women"was under a stairwell. He tapped on the swinging door.

No answer.

"Annie?"He slapped the wood with the flat of his palm. "You in there?"

No answer.

Instead of knocking again, he pushed. The door opened halfway, then swung back hard.

"Go away. You'll get in trouble."

He had found her. Jack pushed again, but the door slammed back. She wanted a couple inches of wood between them.

The girl inside said, "You're so dumb."

The boy outside said nothing. He agreed.

"You'll get in trouble for coming here, but won't stand up for yourself in class."

"I don't even know who said it."

"That's great. Now you've got to show everyone."

"Tell me how and I'll do it."

"Just leave me alone."Annie's voice stiffened. "I don't want to talk anymore."

And she wouldn't.

The silence left Jack with nowhere to go. He trudged into the schoolyard, his mind sorting out choices, adding up possibilities. How could he face the class again? He had no answer for the chipmunk voice.

His feet turned away from school. He walked like a zombie through the parking lot. The asphalt ended. Farm dirt comforted his toes, feeling like home. The cement of civilization was left behind. Soon he was to the bougainvillea and finally, utterly alone. He was running away again.

Memories whisked through his head like spooks through doors at a haunted house. He pictured Sijohn strutting through the yard, crewcut tilted up in pride. Just a short dumpy coach fixated on teamwork. Someone who gained height from high-heeled boots

and class from three-piece suits and most important-
ly, attitude, Sijohn knew who he was. He knew what
he wanted and he wasn't afraid to show that to everyone. Another spook clouded into Jack's brain. It was
his mother, chin out, blasting at Broomhead. She could
have backed down to the boss, run away from trouble.
People like Broomhead counted on that.

His mother and Sijohn—an unlikely pair to pop into
his head. They were opposite, except neither knuckled
under. Man or woman, in high heeled boots or rippled
soles, you have to have enough guts to be yourself, not
part of some crowd. Jack turned around without actually deciding to do it. Just like he hadn't decided to flip
the pot out the bus window. He wouldn't back down
again if he had a chance to make a stand. But he didn't
know how, or even if he'd get a chance.

Chambers' class was quiet when he entered. No one
talked at all, chipmunk or human. Annie was back like
nothing happened. She gave him a long look. In fact,
everyone did. For perhaps the last time, Jack was the
star attraction.

Chambers gazed down from the control-tower desk.
The teacher had finally made it to class. She opened a
drawer, fingering a detention pad. Indecision squeezed
her eyes together.

Finally, she dropped the pad, and shut the drawer.
She pressed a butterfly clip attached to the outside of
the desk. An absence slip floated down. Jack picked it
off the floor and offered it to her. Chambers shook her
head.

Jack wondered if it was mercy or pity. This *was*

game day. More likely, though, the teacher was protecting her own backside. If she'd been there, none of this would've happened. He crumpled the slip into trash and took his seat just as the bell rang.

Instead of rushing out as usual, the class stayed in their seats and watched him leave. Jack made a solo walk out the door. Then the room buzzed like a bee hive whopped by a sharp stick.

Jack heard it through the opening, not knowing if it was about the fact he left or the fact he came back. His classmates dispersed with a fury into the yard. They had stories to tell.

The call for ballplayers went over the PA during fifth period. The team left pridefully, rubbing it in to the average citizen stuck behind in class. The gym brought sobriety. Small talk petered out as they suited up. Jack taped his ankle and draped the blue tank top over his shoulders for a final time. He climbed the stairs two at a time but found the gym empty.

Or almost empty. The cheerleaders had staked territory in front of the home stands. Annie and Tara and Grace covered the middle quadrant, the home cheering section once school was out. Jack searched Annie's face but couldn't read it.

Sijohn made it to the top of the stairs as the squad divided for lay ins. Jack sank his first, slapping right hand on backboard coming down. His ankle ached as he got into the rebound line. The coach waved Jack over.

"Can you jump?"

Jack nodded.

"Can you shoot?"

Jack nodded again.

"Get back in line." He looked at the tape barely visible out of Jack's sock. Sijohn fingered his lapel, backing up until he felt the bench hit his knees.

Jack wanted to show just how healthy he was. He muscled into the shooting line and waited impatiently for his turn. Finally, it came. Jamal dropped a bounce-pass waist-high. Jack scooped it up and soared for the rim. His hand fell short of metal but brushed net. The ball went in. The coach dropped his lapel and leaned forward. He sat on his hands to keep them still.

There was commotion as a class of students entered the gym. The boys and girls were antsy and small, probably freshmen. Jack glanced at the clock to see if school had let out. It hadn't. Who were these people, then? The answer was at the end of the line.

Mr. Martinez, arching an eye over his rascally homeroom, brought up the rear. Half-glasses, suspended by a black rubber strap, bounced against his chest. A briefcase, fat and beat-up, dangled from a hand. Disgusted with Jack or not, the teacher was keeping his promise.

Martinez's homeroom took squatters' rights to the best seats—dead center, home side. Annie and Tara huddled in front of them, negotiating rights to the mini-mob. Annie was bigger and she won.

The class whooped at her, but it wasn't enough to disturb their teacher. Martinez had already popped open the briefcase. His head went behind it to retrieve papers. He stacked them on his lap, retracting reading glasses up by a black strap. The frames were adjusted on his nose. An essay was selected and pulled within focusing distance. He went about the business of being an English teacher, oblivious to hoots and howls around him.

Layups changed to jumpers. The solitary homeroom applauded makes, groaned over misses. Jack missed, received a groan, and headed back to rebound.

A woman, dressed in blue scrubs hovered at the far entrance. She hesitated uncertainly for a moment, then stepped boldly out onto the gym floor.

CHAPTER 40

EVEN HER SMALL backpack was blue. She walked with the slight stoop of someone who makes a living on her feet. The rectangular border around the playing floor made her stop.

Her foot was in the green paint of the out-of-bounds line. She retracted it carefully. She might not know basketball, but she could respect a boundary.

The right side of the gym applauded as Jamal swished a shot. The woman in blue looked left. The stands were still deserted on that end. She toddled uncertainly, made up her mind, then pivoted with military precision. Gaining momentum with each stride, she marched down the empty flank. Jack turned his back to the basket to watch her. His mother had never been to a game before.

Not there, he pleaded silently. Sit anywhere but there.

His mother climbed up three rows, smack dab in the Ventura cheering section. At the exact center seat, she executed another military turn. Lining up directly across from Martinez's homeroom, Mrs. Marston plopped down.

Jack winced. At least she could embarrass him from the right section.

Someone tapped him and he spun around. A pass bumped off the floor and caught him on the little finger. He unleashed a sorry-looking jumper as the finger throbbed. Martinez's animals groaned when the ball caromed off the hoop. A string of five baskets in a row had been broken.

The negative feedback annoyed Annie. She peeked at Jack and he looked at her. His eyes scanned down her neck. She wore the usual outfit: tight blue sweater with a "K" across the chest, pleated skirt ending mid-thigh, blue and white running shoes.

She saw him wave to the lonely spectator. When the woman waved back, Jack jerked a thumb to the Kennedy side of the gym. The spectator thought it mere greeting and waved harder. Jack gave up and joined the rebound line. Annie's eyes, curious now, stayed on the woman in blue.

Sijohn clapped his hands twice. The two lines merged toward the exit. Annie agitated the mini-mob into a farewell cheer. The team pounded down stairs. The boys spread out on benches to wait for Sijohn's entrance. Banter faded to silence. The coach dallied topside, letting them stew in their own nervousness.

Meanwhile, a dark yellow bus rolled into the Kennedy yard. Double belts of purple paper banners corrupted the normal, orange school bus. One belt roped under a window. Another draped lengthwise down the roof like a purple stripe on an orange skunk.

The sanctity of academia was shattered by the screech of air brakes. The bus stopped forward progress, rolling back a foot. Behind school walls, students halted the pursuit of knowledge and cocked their ears.

A hand brake ratcheted. A key clicked. The engine quit. Voices took over, amplified by the bounce of tin wall acoustics.

"Ventura"

"Ventura"

"Ventura"

The bus door lurched open with a gaseous hiss. The prisoners inside made a break for freedom. They, too, were decorated purple. Purple sashes and pants and shoelaces. Purple skirts and hats and shirts. Large purple sunglasses and jackets and sweaters.

The voices faded as the visitors funneled toward the gym. Teachers sighed. Twenty minutes to go. They thought of salvaging lesson plans. Before thoughts became actions, another vehicle desecrated the silence. This one had purple hubcaps. The Kennedy teachers gave up.

The gang from the first bus entered the gym. They found a middle aged trespasser in the center section. A girl at the head of the line asked her to move. The woman in blue ignored the request. Her chin came out a little.

A letterman wormed out of the pack. He rephrased it as an order. Mrs. Marston's chin became more pronounced. Finally, an adult chaperon emerged from the line. A purple necktie swished out of his sport coat.

"Excuse me,"the man said. His tie ticked like a pendulum on a grandfather clock.

The homesteader didn't answer.

To heighten his authority, the chaperon decided to wait for his tie to stop rotating. When it did, he said, "You're in the wrong seat. This is the student cheering section."

Annie, from across the gym, guessed what was happening. She said something to Martinez's group. The homeroom answered in high freshman voice. The cheerleader waved a hand for silence so she could listen.

Jack's mother made a concession. Too make more room, she picked her small backpack off the bench. She hugged it to her stomach like a teddy bear. It wasn't enough for the chaperon. He wanted her out and was willing to get tough. He barked:

"You don't belong here."

Mrs. Marston peered at him his tie was rotating again. Her hands tightened on the small backpack. The chin thrust out stubbornly. She was there first. People like this didn't tell her what to do. Not anymore. Voices from the purple line cracked orders at her:

"Move it, old lady."

"You dried up old prune."

"Get on your own side."

A boy in high-top shoes chortled something nasty

between his teeth. The chaperon tried to hush him. He flapped his arms up and down like a large bird trying to take off.

The pantomime looked ridiculous to the homeroom across the way. Annie's arm raised like she was holding a starter's gun at a track meet. Martinez's homeroom got ready.

The purple man had enough. This lady was nothing more than a trespasser. With the swishing, he grabbed Jack's mother. The nurse tried to shake him off, but felt herself raise off the seat.

Annie's arm dropped. A blast of controlled noise scorched out of Martinez's homeroom. "Don't move!" Two words boomed across the floor with the impact of a loud firecracker.

The purple man went stiff, like a flashbulb had caught him in a criminal act. Even his necktie paused, pointing down like an arrow at his dubious deed.

Annie spun around to see if the cheer had worked.

It had. The matter had gone public. The chaperon might as well toss an orphan into a storm. His hand weakened on the nurse's arm. Mrs. Marston' shook away the fingers with affronted dignity, as if shedding a mugger's grope.

The Ventura fans sensed defeat and dribbled into the cheering section. The purple man stood for a moment like a rock in a stream. Soon he recognized the inevitable and followed them in. He wasn't happy. In less than a minute, Jack's mother was a dot in a sea of purple. She bent over her backpack in a tight blue ball, elbows out and ready just in case.

The Kennedy lot had filled with dark yellow buses with purple streamers. More visitors flooded the gym. Soon the left side was solid as a spring field of purple wildflowers. The overflow, with nowhere to go, spilled across the floor to the right side of the gym.

Martinez's homeroom frowned at the newcomers. The interlopers huddled together in pockets of safety. They were barely seated when their team came out on the floor. The chant of "Ventura"began again in earnest. A bell buzzed through the gym, drowning out the chant.

School was out for Kennedy. Students streamed out of homerooms like horses out a starting gate. They grumbled when they entered the gym, though. The left side was packed with visitors—far enough. But a patchwork purple also dotted the right side, the home side. Nothing to be done about it, possession being nine points of the law.

Kennedy took the seats left. The gaps filled with hometown fans, like cement around bricks in a purple chimney. Except for Martinez's homeroom, the rooters were more scattered than unified. Doorways overflowed with standing room only.

Darrin used his state-of-the-art camera as a passport to the playing floor. He kibitzed with Annie, teasing her about something before she finally shooed him away.

The rumbling overhead could be heard by the boys in the locker room. The training room door opened. Sijohn entered. Eric's head went below the bench like an ostrich hiding from trouble. The coach waited. The rest of the eyes came up. For the umpteenth time, the coach repeated the magic word.

"Teamwork. Play for each other and you win. Play for yourself and you lose."

That was it in a nutshell—nothing more to say. He flicked dismissal. Jack passed by Ryan, who looked pale and shakey. They walked up the stairs—no energy to waste with the game so near.

Wall-to-wall purple greeted them when they hit the floor. This was crazy—a home game that wasn't.

Jack scanned the Ventura cheering section for reassurance. A blue lady bear-hugged a backpack between two purple rooters. Though squashed and barely visible, his mother was still there.

Kennedy split into two lines again. They passed by Martinez's homeroom. Annie had them on their feet. Mr. Martinez was ignoring the noise, still correcting papers.

Jack pushed the leather ball against his palm just like in practice. The pinkie still ached, though not bad. The only soreness was a twinge when his little finger pressed the ball. He adjusted his grip to lighten the pressure, but doing so altered the ball's rotation. His soft touch hardened. Marginal "bounce around"shots fell off instead of in. He lined up for another foul shot. The students in the doorway counted every time a ball went through. Darrin, holding camera overhead, pushed to the front and set up under the basket. Jack's turn came after three in a row. Darrin pointed the camera at him like a gun.

Jack crouched, snapped his wrist. The ball hit the

heel of the rim, went straight up three feet, then down through the hoop. Not pretty, but the crowd at the door yelled, "Four." The camera did not flash, not this time for a practice shot that didn't count.

On the way to the end of the line, Jack peeked at Ventura. He searched for Sterling. He was a reminder of Jack's failures in soccer—and found him easily. There'd been too many scissor kicks in too many dreams. The body was different than Jack remembered, though. Arms long, hands big, but on a frame more rangy than tall. The face had a faint five o'clock shadow. Sterling was more man than boy, like his hormones had gotten a head start.

There was commotion by the front door—another person muscled through the crowd. The invader was too short to have his head visible over the pack, but an arm raised to the ceiling as if calling for attention. It was sheathed in black leather.

CHAPTER 41

GRANT PUSHED THROUGH the crowd and climbed up the Kennedy side. The seats were filled. He nudged the boy at the end of the top row anyway. One look at the college man was enough for the boy. He shoved the girl next to him. A ripple ran down the row like a caterpillar taking multiple strides. A space materialized where none existed.

It fits, Jack thought. His mother was in the middle of a cheering section, but the wrong cheering section. His brother was in the right cheering section, but on the edge looking in.

Grant's eyes were too distant to read. If he watched the warmups, there was no indication. If he noticed a dot of maternal blue across the floor, there was no wave. Jack brought a hand up in greeting. The leather sleeves folded into each other.

The clock on the scorer's table hit zero, buzzing like an amplified kitchen timer. End of playtime, beginning of real time. Jack took his old seat at the end of the bench.

The purple yell leaders across the way were mostly male. Sweaters were carefully rolled to showcase biceps. The boys looked ready to pump iron, not lead cheers. The one girl cheerleader was small like Tara. The Kennedy starters gathered around the coach and blocked Jack's view. Sijohn said to the huddle:

"Box and one. Deny the ball."

The clock on the scorer's table buzzed again. The coach's stubby hand went out, palm up. If the team needed much instruction now, they were in trouble.

Palms piled on top of palms. The starters said "hey"in unison and broke the totem of flesh. Sijohn backed up to the bench and collapsed. His team went forth to meet the enemy.

Dereck entered the jumping circle, as did a tree trunk center four inches taller. The ref didn't bother to bounce the ball for rhythm, but tossed it right up. Both centers were thrown off a fraction. The ball flopped off Dereck's shoulder toward Jared. Instead of calling a re-jump, the ref let it go.

Jared grabbed the ball tight, razor blade swinging on gold chain. Everyone backed off. Annie launched the first cheer. Martinez's homeroom put their lungs into it, but the teacher himself saw no reason to close his briefcase. There were papers to grade.

Tara joined in, but her spread out constituency didn't. She drifted toward those who did respond—the entrance packed with latecomers. The doorway and homeroom united like stereo speakers, but weak stereo from a garbled station. Tara tried to twist the volume up, but the bodies in the gym sponged up the noise. The cheer had a faintly neutral quality, which was fitting for a home game that wasn't.

"Score."

"Score."

"Score."

Dereck took it as command. A pass from Jared arched into a little skyhook. The ball rippled through the net. The center dashed back with fist raised, then opened it to slap Jared's palm Sijohn cupped his hands into a megaphone as they scuttled by the bench.

"Box and one!"

Jared had already picked up his man. A tight box set up behind him. The Ventura player cut left, cut right; Jared stuck on his hip like a gymnast. The player looked at the ref for help against hand checks, but there was no call. The best players from each team would be allowed to go at each other.

Finally, the guard quit looking for the star player. The tree trunk center rolled through the unpopulated zone. He took a high pass and wheeled into a clumsy imitation of a skyhook. The ball skidded off metal into Dereck's hands. The players went the other way.

There was only one visiting female yell leader. The lone girl, dainty and cute, stood still under pompom—mere decoration. The musclemen compensated by gyrating. Three cartwheels and two flips later they exhorted:

"Get that ball."

An avalanche of noise rumbled through the gym.

Kennedy's puny response was buried in decibels. The question of cheering dominance was settled. Ventura had the numbers and they were organized. Out on the floor, however, there was still equality.

Ventura shuttled in combinations of players in order to break the impasse. Only Sterling never came out—he was the main man. If anyone could break the game open, he was the one. Kennedy did not substitute—they were happy to stay close. A sub might shatter team chemistry. The half ended in a virtual stand-off, Kennedy finally one up.

Sijohn didn't say much at halftime. They were playing the best team in the league even up and the coach said, "One more half."

They passed the coach, climbed the stairs, found the gym smoking. A purple pyramid had been constructed at center court. The most muscular yell leaders composed the base of the triangle. At the apex, four body-lengths up, the lone female cheerleader wobbled.

A shriek vented through her clenched teeth as the pyramid tipped forward. She toppled into safe, muscle-bound arms. The third story crumbled next, then second. The boys bounced off the floor effortlessly like it was a trampoline.

Jack circled the debris from the collapsed human structure. The girl was set gently down. She picked up a pom-pom. She stood still. She didn't bounce or scream or kick, but seemed to pose for a nonexistent camera.

She was undeniably good to look at and light to lift. But she didn't lead cheers. That wasn't in her job description. Jack snuck a peek at the jumping Annie. He decided he was old-fashioned. He liked watching the girls cheer.

Jack also checked for his mother. She sat like a dainty blue center in petals of purple. The boosters stood up, obscuring her view. He thought, that's OK—there's nothing to see. His brother was there, too, arms still folded. Everyone was in the gym that Jack cared about. Jack chafed on the bench. The stage was set. He ached to go in, ached to show them all. Ventura made a minor strategy change for the second half. Sterling switched men so he could guard Jared. The result was apparent as soon as Kennedy grabbed the tip-off. Sterling clamped hands onto the captain just as Jared did to him. Eric looked right, the way he always did, but Jared was covered.

Six times the ball went up the floor, and six times Jared didn't lay a hand on it. Finally, he had enough, and slapped a hand check away. Sterling reattached the hand. The boy-man from Ventura wasn't afraid of Jared, razor blade or not. The captain slapped it away again.

The whistle blew. Sterling went to the line. Sijohn yelled some abuse, but the ref was evidently hard of hearing. Jared argued, but it was hypocritical. He'd been whacking Sterling all game. Now he had to take some of his own medicine. If you dished it out, you had to take it. Ventura went ahead on the freethrow.

Jared loosened up on his prey the next time down. The Ventura star got a pass inside. He rammed home a short hook shot. On the other end, Jared also found himself open for a pass. The captain snagged it and pushed inside. Sterling blocked the key, but sagged back to allow an outside shot. It counted two points all the same.

A gentleman's agreement was struck. Jared's basket verified both parties could profit. Boundaries for the second half were re-established.

Defensive pressure would loosen away from the ball. Sterling would not be overplayed against the pass. In return, the captain was allowed the same courtesy. Jared would be allowed outside shots, allowed to fatten his average. The two stars would get their points. It would look good in the papers.

There was a problem. Sterling was better. Once he had the ball, he did damage. He had demolished Colonna. He had stuffed Robeson. Jared might exceed his average, but Sterling would get more. Kennedy might come close, but they'd lose the game. Jared would be permitted certain tricks to play the crowd, but not enough of them to win.

It would be a respectable defeat. Instead of hanging tough, they'd hang close—right to the end when Ventura would eke out a predictable victory. Jared would get his points. They'd all get their points. Kennedy would just lose to a better team. Nobody's fault. A good show but not good enough. Second place in basketball... nothing more.

The change in the game was too gradual to be noticed, except on the scoreboard. The numbers drifted slowly apart; two points, four points, six points. When Sijohn signaled Eric to call time it was all sevens—seven points down with seven minutes left. Jamal turned to Jack and said:

"Listen."

"For what?"

"Your name."

They both looked at Sijohn's face, which was starting to slide behind fingers. This could not go on much longer.

Jack leaned backwards and flexed his ankle. It felt strong but rigid beneath the tape. He looked at Jamal. He looked at Sijohn again, and his eyes stayed there.

The cheerleaders built another pyramid.

In the corner of the top row, Grant refolded his arms.

The English teacher continued to mark papers.

A nurse sat inconspicuously in standing room only.

The coach's face continued to slide until it was hidden behind stubby fingers.

Sijohn's face finally came out from behind the hands. He walked to the end of the bench. On the way, he tapped Jack on the knee.

"In for Jared."

Time was called. Jack took the long walk to the scorer's table. His heart drummed like a hot-blooded bird trying to stay cool. The announcement was made over the PA.

CHAPTER 42

THE PYRAMID COLLAPSED.

Up in the last row. Grant's arms unfolded.

Mr. Martinez glanced up from an essay.

Across the floor, his mother directed a boy in front of her to sit down.

Annie turned sideways, ignoring the homeroom for a second.

Jack turned around from the scorer's table. Instead of being surrounded, Sijohn was still alone. Ten paces away, the players had set up their own huddle. Jared was in the center of it, where the coach should be. The starters were waiting for the coach to join them.

Sijohn would have none of that. They'd join him or they'd sit. The coach stood ramrod straight, tall as only short men can be.

Jack went by the bench. He reached for a towel even though the only sweat he had was cold and long dry. He draped the towel on his skull like an upside down "U".

He paused in front of Jamal. Jack spoke through the folds of the towel so nobody could see his lips move.

"Listen."

"For what?" Jamal said.

"Your name."

He dumped the towel off his head. Without a blink, Jack bypassed his peers in the huddle. Jared's burning gaze lashed against his back.

Dereck followed Jack's lead and peeled away from Jared's makeshift huddle. The big center marched ten deliberate paces until he was next to Sijohn. The betrayal shattered Jared's unity, and Jack was reminded of the tussle at Annie's party. Moe and Ryan and Eric followed Dereck. Only the captain was left, by himself.

Jared's year was over. Fifty percent from the field, perfect from the line, washed up for the day. He'd be lucky if Sijohn let him sit on the bench. No way to end a season, or a career. He was just an observer in uniform. The time-out buzzer droned. Jared loitered on the sideline another minute. He had little choice but to fill the hole left by Jack. The rebel hit the bench. Rearend slammed down, legs sticking out defiantly. The sideline drama went mostly unnoticed, except Annie never stopped looking.

The visitors thought Kennedy had thrown in the towel. If someone else could guard Sterling why hadn't he played before?

With seven minutes to league championship, their attitude was, "Wake me when it's over." Even Ventura fans turned quiet, satisfied with the trend of the game.

Kennedy was even quieter. Nothing to cheer about, especially with the captain gone.

But the crowd didn't boo Jack—they watched him. The fans semi-hushed as the gossip spread through the stands like a blanket unfolding. It was like someone had returned from the dead. Those who knew the story pointed at the runaway who'd come back.

Jack hit the floor to begin the most important eight minutes of his life. He knew exactly where to go—he wanted to guard Sterling. That's the way it had to be. The Ventura star tagged a hand onto Jack's trunks. They'd guard each other.

The ref released the ball to Dereck out of bounds. When the center slapped the ball, Jack took off. A pass lofted high overhead. Jack whipped down the sideline, leaving the purple star in the dust. Sterling yanked on Jack's trunks to slow him down. It was enough to spoil the timing. The ball was slapped down for an interception.

"C'mon, Jack,"someone screamed in the quiet gym.

"It wasn't my fault,"Jack felt like yelling back. He waited for a whistle that didn't come. He was playing with the big boys now. Jack was faster, quicker, but not as strong as the boy-man guard. He needed the calls.

He looked to Sijohn for help. The coach's hands slid back over his face. The attempted rebellion had taken something out of the man who preached teamwork. The indomitable coach was wounded. Time was running out without a fight.

Jack had to show everybody, including the coach. He'd play by the rules, or lack of them, that the refs enforced. He picked up at half court, overplaying like Jared had done at the start of the game. Sterling pushed the skinny arms away.

Jack reapplied them. They were slapped away again. Once more they reattached. The next time they were punched away. Again they came back.

This time it was Sterling who looked for official help. The whistle didn't even enter the ref's mouth. Hand-checks were illegal but calling them was ticky-tack. Minor fouls would slow down the game. Jack's hands affixed again to the Ventura star's hips.

The purple point guard decided not to force the pass and risk an interception. The tree trunk center had no such problems being open on the other side of the floor. Sterling scowled at the opportunity missed. There'd be no gentlemen's agreement with Jack.

The tree trunk took it to the hoop. The ball skidded off, and Moe kicked the rebound out to Ryan. Jack streaked ahead of Sterling. The pass was perfect. Jack checked into the scoring column with two easy points.

On the way back, Jack searched for his family. The crowd was still comatose. One spot of blue in the purple cheering section stood up, but she was pulled down again. His mother was alive and well. Annie, Tara and Grace tried to start a cheer going, but it trailed off and died. Sijohn's fingers spread and he peeked between them.

Jack started his defense at the half court line, although his teammates didn't. Crouching low, he glued his eyes to Sterling's waist. Head-fakes didn't work if they weren't seen. His feet moved with Ventura's forward's feet.

Finally, the ball handler gave up on the star. The pass went to the other forward, who immediately aced a shot from the corner. As Jack pivoted to screen off the rebound, an arm jolted him backwards. Whistles blew.

"Number eighteen, you're on his back,"the official announced. That was Sterling's number, but Jack wasn't waved to the line. Instead, Dereck was picked to shoot.

Jack knew it was a mistake. He consoled himself that a foul was finally called, but he missed having a moment in front of the crowd. He had something to prove. Images raced through his head: Grant, Annie, Jared, all the faceless people in the stands who didn't believe in him.

Jack had one basket, and time was running out. He wanted to win; he wanted to be a hero. He could have both. Crossing in front of Annie he drifted to the bench for a towel.

He felt his shoulder blades constrict with an involuntary shiver. Annie followed Jack's eyes to Jared. He was slouched on the end of the bench glaring. The captain's eyes smoldered like coals in a spent fire.

Jack dropped the towel and turned away. This was no time for a staring match. Martinez's homeroom resurrected a little after Dereck's foul shots went down. A weak cry went up.

"Defense."

Unable to get inside, Ventura passed the ball

around the perimeter. The clock was on their side. The ball control offense continued. Pass after pass went nowhere. The crowd started to get bored—the cheer from Martinez's homeroom died out. Nobody believed the game could be won, especially if the visitors stalled. The clock ticked down.

Sterling was hungry for the ball. Jack eased up on the pressure, hoping to lure a pass inside. The point guard took the bait. Jack lurched forward as the pass came, stretching to deflect it.

The ball careened toward the purple cheering section with Jack in hot pursuit. He dove just before the out-of-bounds line, knees burning against the floor. The ball suctioned under his palm, barely in-bounds.

"Time out!"Jack screamed.

The words were audible in the quiet gym, but the refs had been lazy—they were out of position to call it. Before a whistle could sound, Sterling's heavy body hammered into Jack. The ball wrenched free. Sterling trapped it with an arm before it could roll out of bounds. Sterling sprang to his feet triumphantly, waving his prize overhead. The edge of his heel, by just a millimeter, encroached into the painted line. The Ventura cheering section hushed at the sin being committed right in front of them.

A figure in blue rose up like a Phoenix out of purple flames. She might not know basketball but she could respect a boundary. In the hushed cheering section, in the suddenly silent gym, Mrs. Marston shrilled like Broomhead had appeared in front of her.

"He's on the line! His foot's on the line!"

CHAPTER 43

IT WAS THE awe-inspiring, ear-splitting, wake-me-up-on-Saturday-morning voice. The sound peeled through the gym like it was on the speaker system.

Grant stood up in the last row.

Annie maneuvered in front of Martinez's homeroom.

Martinez himself tried to keep a pile of papers from spilling off his lap.

The official had been beaten to the punch by a woman spectator. He sucked in the whistle and blew out his lungs. His striped arm stretched at Kennedy.

"Out of bounds, blue."Jack's time-out was belatedly acknowledged. One noisy lady had forced the officials to do their job.

Sijohn unshielded his eyes at last. But the visiting coach, disgusted, tracked down the ref at the scoring table.

The game was getting close, at least close enough for argument. Jack could hear him grouse about fans doing the officiating.

Like the ref, Mrs. Marston turned a deaf ear to rude comments. The visitors weren't tolerating her presence anymore. Fingers pointed at the Kennedy's side, directing her where she belonged. Jack's mother had influenced the game. Worse than that, she had done it from the very heart of the purple section.

The chaperon stood up, ready to implement the will of the majority. The wayward nurse had cut her own throat. No cheer from Annie could save her now. The man with the purple tick-tock tie slithered toward the woman in blue.

The team circled Sijohn. "Now you're playing the game,"he said. "You've got 'em on the run. Keep it up for one more minute."Dan came up, whispered something, and the coach added, "We're out of time-outs. You've got to finish it."

Jack's knees flamed from the floor-burn. He bent down for a damage report and from the corner of his eye, saw Grant leave the top row and drift down the aisle. Then, from the end of the bench, he felt the hard, bright, hateful eyes burn at him again.

This time his own eyes drilled back into the captain's. No enthusiasm was there, no thought of the team. Jared was full of Jared, no room for anything else.

Jack stood up and went next to the coach. In a soft voice he said, "Jamal."

"What?"Sijohn only heard the "L"on the end. Jamal leaned forward.

Jack said again, still soft, "Jamal."

"Jamal?"Sijohn repeated. Jamal peered down the bench.

Jack didn't answer. Jamal's ears perked up.

Sijohn said louder, "Jamal."

Jack still didn't answer. Jamal got up.

Sijohn repeated, "Jamal?"

"On the way, Coach,"Jamal said. He went by them to the scorer's table. "In for Eric,"he said to the scorekeeper.

The coach's cheekbones rose, pouching up his brown eyes. The mouth crinkled to tight smile. Jack half-smiled back as a reflex. Sijohn looked from Jack to Jamal and back again, remembering a long-ago practice.

"Press,"the coach said. "Press."

Jack was ready to go back to the floor. He had to prove he was a winner. Only one place to do that, and only one way. Grant crossed under the basket as Sijohn whispered a last hoarse message.

"Weave the ball. Everyone touch it before the shot. Play together and you can whip these guys."

Sijohn's eyes came alive as they moved over his five. There wouldn't be any tomorrow if this one got away.

Across the floor, the chaperon hovered next to the nurse. Mrs. Marston sat down abruptly, putting vertical distance between them. The purple man bent over into her face. He tried the evil eye on her, like a strict teacher does to a disruptive student. The nurse averted her head like he had bad breath. The chaperon's temper boiled. He tried to twist into her line of vision.

She refused to look.

His tie began bobbing, as if powered by his hot blood. He wasn't taking no for an answer this time.

Annie and Tara and Grace were busy doing cartwheels in front of the homeroom. The purple yell leaders answered in multiple backflips. The gymnasts flashed cocky smiles of superiority. This feeble attempt to compete with them was amusing. After hours of practice and hours in the weight room, their artistry couldn't be repeated this side of the Olympics.

Ventura's girl yell leader was exempt from the backflip requirement. She did shiver a pom-pom. A college man in leather crossed behind her, unnoticed. With a few jumps, he ascended the stands. He cruised up behind the chaperon.

The adult stumbled back, shocked to find two non-purple human beings in his small world. Grant leaned forward like a boxer at pre-match introductions. A nudge from his chest froze the tick-tock of the purple tie. He said as ominously as he could:

"That's my mother."

The chaperon thought once.

He thought twice.

By the third thought, he was out of there. Discretion was indeed the best part of valor. He ungracefully sidestepped out the aisle.

Grant kicked the knee of the fan adjacent to his mother. The boy made a correct and very quick interpretation. He gently shoved the girl next to him. A chain reaction of shoves caterpillared the stands. An open space somehow materialized in the sardine can row.

Grant reclined next to his mother. Jack's family was unified behind him, although on the wrong side of the gym. In a strange way, he had brought them together.

Mrs. Marston touched Grant's hand with affection. It was nice to have family, to stand with you and even strong enough to enter the enemy stands for one another.

CHAPTER 44

DARRIN SET UP beneath the Kennedy basket. The electronic snaps of his camera were swallowed in noise as he adjusted for light and speed. The referee pushed the journalist back as the buzzer sounded. Three starters plus two add-ons made their way to the floor.

The ball came in and the weave began. Giving Jack some of his own medicine, Sterling overplayed to deny the pass. Everyone else on Kennedy touched the ball, then revolved in a semicircle. Jack nodded to Jamal as he went by. The two second stringers were old practice partners. They knew how to handle an over-aggressive defender.

Jack heard Sijohn holler from the bench. Mrs. Marston seemed to have woken him up reminding him he could make a difference in this game. The ref was yet to be convinced, however. The players should decide this game, not a frivolous call in the last minute.

Jack revolved through the weave until his turn came again. He faked behind Jamal seemingly intent on touching the ball this time. Sterling knew the desperation of a star cut off from glory. He went for the fake.

Jack reversed under Ventura and collected a high floater for an easy two. The gap was closing on the soccer champs.

"Press!"Jack screamed. He jumped to defense, trying to stop Ventura from coming back at them. Jack backed off the ball like he was guarding a zone instead of a man.

He darted just as the ball came inbounds. Knifing in for a steal, Jack bounced off Sterling like a rubber ball. He threw the ball down into a dribble as he lost his balance.

The official wiggled the whistle in his mouth. To avoid the fatal puff of air, Sterling threw his hands back in innocence. The ref bought the act—his cheeks did not inflate.

Jack left them both behind. One player remained between him and two points. It was a guard, small but fast—more trouble for Jack than a big man.

Jack jammed on the brakes and went up for a jumper. It dropped with the automatic efficiency of practice. The crowd erupted, blowing through the commands of the cheerleaders like a hurricane through Miami.

"Press!"Jack bellowed into the din.

Ventura was getting nervous. The guard that Jack had beaten sailed the pass high to the center. He held it with one hand over his head like King Kong. He wheeled away from the pestering mob beneath.

Jamal pressured from the right. To get away from him, the center came down to sea level and dropped the ball into a dribble. Jack flicked his hand in from the left. His opponent retracted like a hermit crab.

When the big man's head turned, Jamal slipped in from the blind side to knock it away. Jack outraced the lumbering center and gained control.

The center finally caught up to him at center court. To redeem his honor, he attempted to steal it back. He was too slow to be a thief, and Jack too fast to let him anyway.

The arm missed the ball and slashed Jack's cheek. The slap left a trail like a second degree burn. The sound galvanized the referee into finally putting air in his whistle.

Sterling, who had been nearby, walked confidently to his own free throw line, ready to shoot. He set up behind the fifteen foot stripe. The rest of the purple followed and took spots along the lane.

Jack stayed at center court next to the referee and watched. Sterling went through a little pantomime like he was shooting a free throw without the ball. It was supposed to activate muscle memory so that the real thing was automatic. He was hoping that the referee heard the slap but was out of position again and didn't see the play.

Jack turned his cheek to the ref and displayed the red mark across it.

"One shot,"the referee said immediately, his voice suddenly audible. Irritated by the hoax, he shooed Sterling away from the line. They went to the other end. After the purple men had their new places, the ball was put gently into Jack's palm.

Darrin had muscled his way just beyond the out of bounds line. The electronic eye of a camera focused on the shooter's chest. As Annie and Tara and Grace flapped their arms down for silence, the lens twisted into focus. The cacophony faded down to snorts and coughs.

The ball was tossed from hand to hand. The jammed little finger hurt where it pressed leather. Jack prolonged the drama with two unnecessary dribbles.

The audience was ready for a swish from the man who never missed. The shot went up without proper rotation, like a knuckleball. It hit the front of the rim, twirled, and dropped. Blessed by luck, his string was alive. A flash of white light froze Jack's reaction as the ball twisted through the cord. He was sticking his tongue out.

The starters from both teams were tired. Jack sucked in a second wind when Jamal swiped the inbounds pass. With an instant switch to offense, Jack freed himself for another deuce.

The game everyone had given up on was tied.

This time Ventura made sure of the inbounds pass. Sterling brought it up the floor himself. Jack annoyed him like a mosquito searching for a place to land and draw blood.

Instead of running the clock down, the Ventura star lost his temper. He slapped the hand off his rump and drove for the basket. Jack closed the lane. Sterling stepped back for a jumper to win the game. The ball hit the heel of the rim and fell off.

Jack charged for the rebound, but right into the sharp elbow of the tree trunk center. Sijohn shot off the bench. Jack was doubled over, speared in the ribs.

"How about a call, ref?"

"My man's hurt!"

"You're a zero, ref, a zero!"

The game went on. A reaching hand tipped the ball to Kennedy. Jack tried to run back, but stumbled out of control. Jamal saw something was wrong, and delayed the dribble.

Jack tried to suck air down his windpipe. A little oxygen trickled in but it was painfully slow, like a kid squeaking air from a pinched balloon.

Sterling freelanced after the ball, not bothering to guard the disabled Jack. It was five against four with Jack out of it.

Sijohn still hadn't cooled down. He bellowed to the ref, "You guys stink."It was almost one sentence too much.

The ref put the whistle in his mouth.

In a softer voice, Sijohn repeated, "You guys stink."He had made his point. No use risking a technical foul that could decide the game. He shadowed his eyes from the lights. The clock said half a minute to overtime.

Martinez's homeroom stayed on their feet, Annie in front of them. Mr. Martinez essays still in hand, looked up with twenty five seconds left. At the twenty second mark, Jamal started the final play.

The pass went to Dereck but Jamal telegraphed it. He didn't see the extra player that didn't have to guard anybody. The freelancing Sterling darted out front for a clean steal.

The Ventura fans went crazy as Sterling accelerated ahead of the pack. He had to go the length of the floor, but it'd be an easy basket. The only person near was the ref, who would not be caught out of position again by a noisy fan.

Sijohn's fingers slid over his face.

Martinez's homeroom was stunned. Annie, unable to get a response, turned around to face the floor.

Jamal, heartsick over his mistake, chased at half-speed. It was a hopeless cause. The layup would be automatic. No way to retrieve the lost pass, or the season that went down the tubes with it.

The Ventura star passed midcourt. The ref trotted behind him like a bodyguard. Sijohn's hands flattened against his eyes, shutting out the reality of defeat. A blue shirt came up behind Jamal apparently serious in contesting the layup everyone else had conceded.

Jack's mother and brother stood up.

Annie dropped her pom-poms.

It was Jack.

CHAPTER 45

IT WAS RIDICULOUS, really. The only player who hadn't given up was gut-sick and way behind. But even though it seemed laughable, Martinez's homeroom was quiet. The boy who wouldn't give up was the same one who always ran away.

The clock ticked down to zero.

Annie brought both hands to her mouth.

Mrs. Marston and Grant were still as statues.

Jack let go of his stomach and forced himself to sprint. It felt like somebody was sticking pins in his belly from the inside.

Jamal gave up and Jack passed him.

Sijohn spread his fingers apart so he could see between them. Sterling had crossed his free throw line. Jack was thirty feet away from the basket—too far away for footsteps to be heard. The Ventura forward lobbed the ball soft against the backboard, a little too soft.

It was just that one out of a hundred layups that

doesn't go cleanly through. The ball danced across the hoop like there was a lid over it. The volume in the purple stands cut down a notch. Jack passed in front of the ref, who seemed surprised to see him.

Sijohn peeked through his fingers, hope rising.

Mr. Martinez grabbed essays firmly in each hand and craned his neck to see through the standing crowd. The ball flagged off the rim, but bounded back to the shooter like a yo-yo. Jack was at the free-throw line when the purple forward sent up a second shot.

Annie stood motionless, hands down, the homeroom forgotten.

Across the floor, Mrs. Marston grabbed Grant and squeezed with all her might.

No doubt about footsteps this time—star players don't miss two in a row. The homeroom erupted in desperate hope as the ball fell off again. Martinez's essays flew out of his hands and spilled like uncut confetti over everyone.

Jack contested the third try. He rammed the purple back, scratching for the rebound, slapping upward with all his power. He felt leather push against his fingertips, pressing his little finger back. Pain spurted through his hand. He hit the floor with a boom felt bone-deep, but not heard at all in the madhouse gym.

From the floor, Jack saw the ball roll around the rim once. Then it rolled around again, losing momentum, like it had a mind of its own, trying to decide, win or lose...

The ball stood still on the edge of the rim, and

finally made up its mind. It toppled into the net.Mr. Martinez's rose through the fluttering essays. The half glasses tumbled off his nose and hung on black rubber. Jack had tipped the ball into the wrong basket. He had scored the winning two points for Ventura!

CHAPTER 46

THE WHISTLE COULD hardly be heard in the bedlam. The ref was moving his arms back and forth, cancelling out the basket. He wouldn't be shown up this time by a screaming woman fan or a short coach. He'd call the foul.

Jack sat up with a start. A foul before the shot—the game was still tied!

Martinez's homeroom let out a whoop. Kennedy was still alive. Mr. Martinez let the English essays float free, not even trying to retrieve them.

The scoreboard removed the accidental points. The purple crowd groaned, but Jack felt a whole lot better. His gut didn't even hurt anymore. Trying to rise from the hardwood, he pushed on the floor with his right hand. A new spasm of pain shot through the little finger. He ignored it and rolled to his left side.

He scanned for the black leather and blue cotton patches in the purple. His mother and Grant were still standing, hugging each other. Jack looked overhead.

Two seconds to go.

Sijohn folded his arms, satisfied afoul had been called. Who says arguing doesn't pay? He went to the edge of the painted sideline. The whistle had blown, which was better than nothing, but it might only be a reprieve. He stared out at the floor, eyebrows arching into a fierce arc.

The ref turned away, trying to ignore him. Sijohn stalked the sideline. When he reinvaded the referee's line of vision, the official looked away again. The game would be decided by a foul shot, but who would shoot?

Grant and his mother strained forward. The purple section around them sat down. The ref had made a call that would decide the game. He prolonged the decision.

Sterling decided to save the official another puff on the whistle. After all, Jack had bashed him, not the other way around. He strode to the free throw line, eyes wide, innocent as a teenager who shaves can be.

He positioned his toes precisely on the fifteen foot stripe. His wrist flicked a motor-rehearsal foul shot. The little pantomime was the straw that broke the camel's back.

The ref was sick of being influenced. He wouldn't be told what to do by a player. The ref pointed to the opposite foul line.

"Foul on purple. Twenty-five to the line."

The Kennedy crowd exploded. The roar doubled when they realized Jack was shooting, the man who never misses. The sound finally ebbed off into a little satisfied sigh.

Walking down to the basket, Jack waggled his shooting hand. He worked the finger like a puppeteer with a broken string.

"You OK?"Dereck interrupted the self-diagnosis.

Jack fisted the hand, nodding without thinking. His little finger was curved like the top of a question mark. He tried to shake the pain out of it. Even if his hand hurt, he could still shoot a free throw. He looked at the two seconds left. One more time, he thought.

A fast blister of noise greeted Jack as he reached the line. He scuffed on the paint. His chance to be a hero had finally arrived. He thought of Chamber's class, the ridicule of the chipmunk voice. He could erase all the mockery forever with one free throw.

The purple gang spread the word for silence. Kennedy had no choice but to follow suit. Jack's mother and brother sat down and hunched forward. Sijohn retreated back to the bench and his hand shadowed his eyes.

Jack bounced the ball once, twice. There was a stab of pain when his little finger pressed the ball. He adjusted his grip to lighten the pressure. His body lowered.

He cleared his mind and concentrated on the front of the hoop. This was something he knew how to do. When his finger flexed, there was another stab. Not a sound could be heard in the gym.

CHAPTER 47

STERLING STEPPED IN front of the referee and screamed in Jack's face:

"Time out!"

To heat up the pressure, they'd give number 25 some time to think. Jack jiggled his arm on the way back to the huddle. The pinkie's second joint, the one close to the fingernail, was already swollen.

He wished the time out was over. The words in his heart he didn't want to say. But now, with this extra time to think, he couldn't seem to hold it back.

"Somebody else shoot it."

"What?"Dereck didn't believe his ears.

"My finger's dislocated."

The huddle of players gaped at him. A second before, Jack was set to shoot, bad finger and all.

"What are you telling me?"Sijohn asked.

Jack looked away. He saw Jared's small mean eyes

on the end of the bench. At least he knew what first string wasn't. It wasn't what others thought of him at all. It was what he thought of himself. When you get down to it, you alone have to decide what is right. Jack turned back to the coach.

"Let Jared shoot it."

Sijohn started to shake his head but stopped. He looked at Jack with respect, the respect due a man taking a last stand. Jack was putting the team first. He had found his own way to win.

"It makes sense, Coach,"Ryan said. "He's the best free thrower left."

"Is that the way you want it?"Sijohn asked.

Jack nodded.

The coach stared at the crooked finger. "Want a doctor?""My mom's a nurse."Jack had seen enough of the hospital. "I'm going home."

Sijohn left the huddle. He had to track down the referee and tell him about the injury.

The captain slipped off his warm-ups. A look of vindication, of glory, shone in his eyes.

"Jack can't come back,"Dan said, "if there's an overtime."

Jack glanced at Jared , who had joined the huddle. "There won't be an overtime,"he said. "Jared'll make it."

Jared's expression said, "You might not be right about much, but you're right about that."

The P.A. announced the change.

Jack's mother said something to Grant, who shrugged his shoulders. Annie, hands on hips, stood off to one side. Jack met their eyes, everyone's eyes, until Jared drew them away like a magnet. He dribbled only once, then straightened his arms. The ball sailed like a frozen rope toward the hoop.

It touched nothing but net.

The crowd detonated like midnight New Years Eve. The benchwarmers leaped to their feet. So did Jack. The visitors were moving upcourt when the buzzer sounded. Kennedy had won by a single point.

Jared's point.

The standees in the doorway combined with Martinez's homeroom went onto the gym floor to make a sandwich of the sweaty blue players. Jared vanished in a circle of students. Then the noose tightened. Jared popped up on top of shoulders. The captain slapped hands extended from below.

Jack was happy, too. His heart beat faintly in his ears. Sweat dripped off his chin. He knew he was part of it, that he had contributed. But he could have been the center of it, in Jared's place.

Jack slipped downstairs unnoticed. He bypassed the shower and just grabbed his sweat suit. Trudging back up the stairs, he envisioned Annie with hands on hips. He thought of the puzzled faces of his mother and brother. He knew what they were thinking—another cop-out.

He told himself it didn't matter. But it did.

Jack peeked into the gym again from the top of

the stairs. Tara was hugging Jamal. Jack saw the little guard's face on the other side of her neck. He was smiling so hard his incisor blank peeked out the far corner of his mouth. He saw Jack looking and mouthed, "thank you"without stopping the embrace.

Jack nodded. Jamal would have been the goat if Jack hadn't saved him.

After saying something to Mr. Martinez, Annie left her station in front of the homeroom. Sijohn stopped talking as she passed the bench. The cheerleader walked toward the visitor's section across the court. The coach followed her across the floor.

Grant and his mother were still in the cheering section. The black leather and blue scrubs were just visible in the unhappy purple fans. Annie was one step into the purple rooters when there was a tap on her shoulder.

It was Sijohn. The coach looked at her hard. He said, "Are you the girl with pink lipstick?"

CHAPTER 48

ANOTHER TIME, ANOTHER day, Jack would be social. But not now. He went downstairs to wash his hands and dry his face. Jack was alone once again. He didn't even look into the gym when he got to the top of the stairs again. He vanished out the back door.

The sun was sliding over the hills. Just into the farm trail, he heard something. Jack stopped his footsteps and listened. A voice filtered through the twilight.

It was a girl's voice.

Jack peered through the bougainvillea bush. There was indeed a girl on the other side, with a boy shorter than she was. She came closer. The short boy shrank back into the twilight.

The girl's skin was faded down a shade by the underexposed sun. But even in reduced light, he could recognize Annie. Her eyes were pinpricks, still adjusting from the brightly-lit gym. Before she could speak, he said, "Don't bother."

She looked at him without understanding.

"You think I blew it."

"You don't know what I think."All the yelling had reduced her voice to a whisper. "I looked for you after the game."

Jack said, "I was there."

"I can't go into the boys' showers. Sijohn said you'd be going home. Jamal showed me the trail."She picked up Jack's hand and squeezed it.

He grimaced.

She compressed it again, very slightly.

Jack thought he suppressed another face.

"It's sore, isn't it?"Her yes went from the hand to his face. "Your finger's really swollen."

Jack didn't answer. He started to blink.

"I know why you didn't shoot."

Jack still didn't answer. The blinks got faster.

"You sacrificed yourself for the team."

Jack shut his eyes to stop the blinking and shook his head.

It's no use, Jack. Sijohn told me what happened. And I told your family."

Jack opened his eyes again.

"Even Ventura knows what you did. Your brother kept hitting people on the back and telling them."The pinprick pupils blotted wider, dark brown slowly overtaking light brown. "Boy, he has a loud voice...they had to call security to get him out of there."

Jack tried to imagine Grant proud of him instead of the other way around.

"Your mother finally dragged him off."Annie paused. "She said to give you a message."

"You talked to her?"

"Your Mom's hard to miss. She'd make a good cheerleader."

Jack thought of the ear shattering scream.

"She hugged me like I was her daughter."

Before he got too embarrassed she added, "I loved it."

He thought of Annie's own mother, who always forgot to pick her up.

"We were all pretty excited. I guess I didn't understand the message."

"Message?"

"Broomhead..."Annie said. "She's Broomhead's equal. Does that make sense?"

The back of his neck prickled. His mother just wanted to be an equal with everybody else, not some second class citizen. Jack shivered. If she could do it, her son could do it. Annie was waiting for him to say something.

"She got the job,"Jack said.

"Everyone was looking for you. Even Mr. Martinez."

"Martinez?"He remembered the half-glasses gaping through confetti."

Jack had visited before zero period too often. Those

papers were a lot of work.

"The only thing that bothered him was they were already corrected."

Jack smiled. That was the Martinez he knew.

Jack retreated a step, a small step, and Annie took his left hand. Their arms straightened into a bridge, like she'd been spun into a dance routine and stranded. She said over the arch:

"The whole school's going to know."

Jack said, "I don't think so."Even if half believed, the other half wouldn't. Jared would put out his own brand of gossip.

"I'll tell Darrin the truth. He'll write another headline. People believe what they read."

"I don't know,"Jack said. Why wouldn't Darrin print the captain's version? That'd be the popular thing to do.

Annie said matter-of-factly, "You're not the only one who likes me. He's going to at least listen to me."

Jack said nothing. She was still holding his left hand, although an arm length away.

"You know how I love secrets. No one'll know where the story came from. I'll be an undocumented source."

There was a short silence.

"It'll be our secret."Annie's face brightened at the whole idea of it. She looked directly at him.

Jack gazed into the honey-brown eyes. He forgot to blink.

"It's a good story. And it has a happy ending."Annie smiled "Writers love those."

After another silence she added, "Besides, it's the truth. I know you could have won the game yourself. Sijohn told me so. You'll be on the front page again. This time no joke."

Jack said, "The sports section's enough."

"That's up to the editor."She pulled a little on his hand.

Jack wavered, leaning toward her.

Annie said, "We'll see who's upon shoulders Monday morning."

"Power of the media,"Jack ventured.

"Nothing can stop it,"she said. "It can even make heroes..."

"Out of second stringers,"Jack said.

Annie took a step forward. She kissed him lightly on the cheek and stepped back, still holding his hand.

"First string to me"she corrected.

He could have objected, but Jack had enough nobleness for one day. If he was a true candidate for sainthood, he would have told her no.

And his free hand wouldn't have touched her cheek.

CHAPTER 49

JACK REELED HER back in close. The long-distance dance was over. One arm dropped to her waist, then the other. He felt his hands touch behind her back. His fingers locked together and he pulled gently. The clean sweater might get a little dirty.

She didn't seem to mind. The honey-brown eyes closed. His cheeks burned hot—too late to turn back. He'd dreamed about this moment but this was real. He wasn't sure how to proceed. Her eyes were still closed.

Before they could open his face darted forward and he fastened his lips to hers, sweet and sweaty and quick. He pulled back.

Annie's eyes stayed shut for a moment longer, then fluttered open like she wasn't expecting such speed. She put a finger to her lips. Were they smeared? Her eyes fell to the purse hooked over her arm. It slid to her wrist and she fumbled into the handbag.

The kiss had hardly been long enough to smear lipstick. Jack was half embarrassed by his own nerve, half wondering if he'd done it right.

In the bottom of the bag, Annie found her lipstick. Glancing at him, she applied it.

Jack noticed it was pink. She saw him examine her lips. "I'm known for pink lipstick,"she said. He didn't answer, but thought vaguely of Sijohn long ago.

Annie said, "The basketball party's this weekend."

Jack hesitated. "Suppose you've been asked..."the hint of a question in his smile.

Annie bridged the gap between them with a step. Her face looked curious, like she had to find out something. There was a question to ask, but it couldn't be answered in words. Her hand touched the back of Jack's neck. This time it was her idea.

Their lips touched, separated slightly, then touched again. The joining was gentle, not like the rushed kiss Jack had launched. It lasted longer this time, but not long enough.

Annie moved back, but Jack caught her hand. When he slowed the retreat, her eyes closed once more. Her face turned toward him again, but hesitated halfway there.

Jack lunged the distance between them. Their lips collided, almost hard against each other. He felt her withdraw at the force of the contact. Her mouth opened and a little sigh escaped, but it wasn't a good sigh.

No, Jack thought, I'm not doing this right.

Annie moved slowly toward him again. Her lips brushed against his, light as wind. When she retreated, she glanced down at her handbag. It was a signal it was over.

But Jack still had her hand. Before she could reach into her purse, he pulled her back close. He moved fast, like a cobra striking, fast like she'd get away, escape. Annie's eyes didn't have time to shut.

Halfway there, Jack finally got it—something clicked in his mind. Sijohn always said he had good instincts. He realized what she'd been showing him.

Jack suddenly slowed himself, put the brakes on. He'd save his speed for the basketball court. When he halted, Annie's eyes blinked at him in wonder. After the third blink they stayed shut.

He forced himself to prolong the moment. Jack knew she wasn't going anywhere. Some things were meant to last. In slow motion, he grazed lightly across the pink lipstick.

If Annie was surprised by the tender stroke, she didn't show it. Her eyes didn't reopen.

With more sureness, Jack caressed her lips again. He stopped, watched for a response, waited for her to retreat.

But Annie didn't withdraw, didn't look down at her purse. Her eyes compressed even tighter. She was waiting, waiting for him.

Jack finally shut his own eyes. He touched her lips once more, at first a bare caress. Then he touched them again, not as soft. The change in degree of pressure was too little to measure, too much for her to miss. But Annie didn't back up or look down at the handbag.

With more promise, more passion, Jack kissed her

again. Gradually, in lingering phases, the kiss grew harder, deeper, his idea. It was like a door inside him opened up and everything he wanted to say but couldn't came spilling out. This time he wasn't too quick.

He kissed her like he wanted to do from the first time he walked her home and fell off the porch. It was better than any dream, for in dreams you have to wake up. When he opened his eyes, she was still there.

The new pink lipstick had vanished completely. The honey-brown eyes opened and shut and opened again. Annie was looking at him strangely, with a newness, like she hadn't seen all of him before.

She inhaled a chest full of air and held it in her lungs. It was exhaled consciously, like she had to remind herself to breathe. She seemed to have forgotten about her purse.

Jack inhaled another gulp of air. The deep breath was released in a long sigh, a good sigh. She kept looking at him, with some amazement, but the curiosity was gone. Her head shook back and forth as if she was saying something to herself. Long, dark brown hair danced across her shoulders.

Definitely first string," she whispered.

Jack didn't require any vehicle, motorized or unmotorized, on the way home. His feet were a few inches above the farm trail. He could have walked across Bottoms Up, even the wide end.

CHAPTER 50

JACK DIDN'T KNOW what to expect at school on Monday. He went pretty much unnoticed through his classes. Annie was pulled out of Chamber's before he could talk to her by a girl with a journalism pass.

Outside of class some freshmen looked at him funny, like they were trying to figure him out. Jack thought they were from Martinez's homeroom. Echoes of the victory reverberated around the school like aftershocks of an earthquake.

At the epicenter was Jared. He played the role of hero at breaks and lunch. He and his friends spread their own version of the victory. The captain had won the game. There was no disputing who made the last second free throw, the one that touched nothing but net. Talk to anyone. It was a matter of record.

Then Tuesday came, and with it a special edition of <u>The Outlook</u>. Several preview copies circulated through the school. Jack didn't get a chance to see it, but the story leaked out between classes. One person told another and the tale spread like wildfire. Darrin, always looking for an angle had found one.

He'd written about a boy who sacrificed his own glory for the sake of the team. An undocumented source told the story of a hidden hero, one who was willing to keep the heroics private. The contrast of Jack's reticence next to Jared's bragging was unavoidable.

If you had to choose a version of the truth, it was easy. Maybe Jack wasn't as popular as the captain, but shyness can work in your favor. It's alright to be shy when someone else trumpets your achievement. Besides, the real facts were in print. As Annie said, people believe what they read.

The undocumented source mentioned in the article was a mystery to everyone at Kennedy. But even if the whole school stood in line to ask, Jack wasn't going to tell. After all, it a was mystery if people didn't know the answer.

At break, people went a little crazy trying to guess the undisclosed source behind the story. It could have been anybody on the team, or even someone close to it. Jack's refusal to reveal the secret made everyone more curious.

At lunch he spotted Annie holding a preview newspaper over by the gym. Girls squeezed around her at the picnic table, like she had information to give. Annie let them spy over her shoulder at the paper, but she wouldn't let go of it.

She would not acknowledge the questions flying around her. Her real emotions were barricaded from the swarm at the picnic table. Annie's eyes moved far away, across the yard. Her lips went straight across with no expression. She wasn't going to give it away, her secret...their secret.

Jack couldn't get to her right away. Everyone was pestering him, even people he didn't know. When he tried to move forward, a class got out and poured down the steps. The mob around him got bigger. He'd never get used to being a celebrity. With effort, Jack managed to float the entourage in toward the picnic table.

As he got closer, he realized Annie had been looking at him from across the yard. He could see her face now. Her mouth was pressed into a tight line. Her lips etched straight across in a mask.

He knew the secret was safe. She was ignoring the girls around her and watching only him. Jack locked onto those dark honey brown eyes.

When Annie saw him looking back, her lips released their tension. She stood up, away from the girls. A twist found its way to one corner of her mouth, and then the other. She didn't have to speak.

Slowly, like hoisting a flag, Annie raised up the preview paper. She held it up in two hands over her head. He could see it over all the girls. The whole yard could see it.

The picture on the front page, not the sports section, was of Jack shooting a free throw.

He was sticking his tongue out.

She mouthed the words "I got your back, Jack" and smiled.